Memories from
a Sinking Ship

Memories from a Sinking Ship

Barry Gifford

Seven Stories Press
New York London Melbourne Toronto

Seven Stories Press
140 Watts Street
New York, NY 10013
www.sevenstories.com

In Canada: Publishers Group Canada, 559 College Street, Suite 402, Toronto, ON M6G 1A9

In the U.K.: Turnaround Publisher Services Ltd., Unit 3, Olympia Trading Estate, Coburg Road, Wood Green, London N22 6TZ

In Australia: Palgrave Macmillan, 15–19 Claremont Street, South Yarra, VIC 3141

College professors may order examination copies of Seven Stories Press titles for a free six-month trial period. To order, visit www.sevenstories.com/textbook/ or send a fax on school letterhead to 212.226.1411.

Library of Congress Cataloging-in-Publication Data:

Gifford, Barry, 1946-
  Memories from a sinking ship / Barry Gifford. -- A Seven Stories Press 1st ed.
    p. cm.
  ISBN 978-1-58322-762-6 (cloth : alk. paper)
  ISBN 978-1-58322-875-3 (pbk. : alk. paper)
  I. Title.

PS3557.I283M46 2007
813'.54--dc22

                           2007005184

Book design by Jon Gilbert
Maps by Barry Gifford
Printed in the U.S.A.

9 8 7 6 5 4 3 2 1

ACKNOWLEDGMENTS

Many of the chapters in this book have previously appeared, several in different form, in the following books: *A Good Man to Know* (Clark City Press, Livingston, Montana, 1992); *The Phantom Father* (Harcourt, Brace, New York, 1997); *Wyoming* (Arcade, New York, 2000); *American Falls* (Seven Stories, New York, 2002); *Do the Blind Dream?* (Seven Stories, New York, 2004); and *The Stars Above Veracruz* (Thunder's Mouth Press, New York, 2006).

Some of the chapters appeared, several in different form, in the following magazines, newspapers or anthologies: *The PEN Short Story Collection* (Ballantine Books, New York, 1985), *Arizona Republic*, *San Francisco Chronicle*, *San Francisco Examiner*, *The Fireside Book of Baseball* (Simon and Schuster, New York, 1987), *Speak* (San Francisco), *Post Road* (New York), *Film Comment* (New York), *Confabulario* of *El Universal*(Mexico City), *El Angel* of *La Reforma* (Mexico City), *Narrative* (San Francisco), *Dazed and Confused* (London), *The Independent* (London), *El Pais* (Madrid), *L'Immature* (Paris), *City Lights Review* (San Francisco), *Max* (Milan), *La Repubblica delle Donne* (Milan), *Another Magazine* (London), *Bridge* (Chicago), *Plan V* (Buenos Aires), *Southwest Review* (Dallas), *Flash Fiction Forward* (W.W. Norton, New York, 2006) and *New Sudden Fiction: Short Stories from America and Beyond* (W.W. Norton, New York, 2007).

The author wishes to thank The Christopher Isherwood Foundation for their support during the writing of this book.

For Pops,
Roy's best friend

I . . . have always known that my destiny was, above all, a literary destiny—that bad things and some good things would happen to me, but that, in the long run, all of it would be converted into words. Particularly the bad things, since happiness does not need to be transformed: happiness is its own end.

—Jorge Luis Borges

Contents

A Good Man to Know

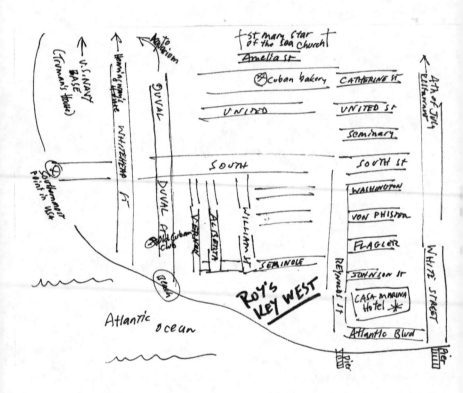

Memories from a Sinking Ship

When Roy was five years old his mother took him to Chicago to stay with his grandmother while she went to Acapulco with her new boyfriend, Rafaelito Faz. Roy had been told that hell was boiling but when he and his mother flew up from Miami and arrived in Chicago during the dead of winter he decided this was a lie. Hell was cold, not hot, and he was horrified that his mother had delivered him to such a place. My mother must hate me, Roy thought, to have brought me here. I must have done something terribly wrong. The fact that his grandmother was there already was proof to Roy that she, too, had committed an unforgivable sin.

Roy's mother stayed in hell only long enough to hand him over. Rafaelito Faz would meet her in Mexico. "He's very rich," Roy's grandmother informed him. "The Faz family owns a chain of department stores in Venezuela." Rich people, Roy concluded, did not have to go to hell. His mother had shown him a picture of Rafaelito Faz clipped from the *Miami Herald*. His hair was parted down the middle and he had a wispy mustache that looked as if it might blow off in the Chicago wind. Underneath the photograph was the caption, "Faz heir visits city."

When Roy's mother returned from her holiday, she was wearing a white coat and her skin was as brown as Chico

Carrasquel's, the shortstop for the Chicago White Sox. Roy did not tell his mother that he was angry at her for dropping him off in hell while she went to a fabulous beach in another country because he was afraid that if he did she would do it again. Roy asked her if Rafaelito Faz had come to Chicago with her. "Forget *that* one, Roy," she said. "I don't ever want to see the rat again."

The next time Roy went to Chicago to visit his grandmother, he was almost seven and it was during the summer. His mother disappeared after two or three days. Roy's grandmother said that she had gone to see a friend who had a house on a lake in Minnesota. "Which one?" Roy asked. "There are 10,000 lakes in Minnesota, Roy," his grandmother told him, "if you can believe what it says on their license plate, but the only one I can name is Superior."

While Roy's mother was in the land of 10,000 lakes, there was a sanitation workers strike in Chicago. Garbage piled up in the streets and alleys. Now the weather was very warm and humid and the city started to stink. Big Cicero, the hunchback with a twisted nose who once wrestled Killer Kowalski at Marigold Arena and now worked at the newsstand on the corner near the house, said to Roy's grandmother, "May they rot in hell, them garbagemen. They get a king's ransom as it is just for throwin' bags. Cops oughta kneecap 'em, put 'em on the rails. The mayor'll call in the troops soon it don't end, you'll see." Roy's grandmother said, "Don't have a heart attack, Cicero." "Already had one," he said.

One afternoon Roy looked out a window at the rear of the house and saw rats running through the backyard. A few of them were sitting in and climbing over the red fire truck his grandmother had bought for him to pedal around the yard and on the sidewalk in front of her house. "Nanny, look!" Roy shouted. "Rats are in our yard!"

His grandmother came into the room and looked out the window. The rats were climbing up the wall. She grabbed a broom, leaned out the window with it and began knocking the rats off the yellow bricks. They fell down onto the cement but quickly recovered and headed back up the side of the house. Roy's grandmother dropped the broom into the yard and slammed the window shut. Rats ran up the windows. Roy thought that they must have tiny suction cups attached to their feet to be able to hold on to the glass. He could hear the rats scampering across the gravel on the roof. A flamethrower would stop them, Roy thought. If the mayor really did call in the army, like Big Cicero said he might, they could use flamethrowers to fry the rats. Roy closed his eyes and saw hundreds of blackened rodents sizzling on the sidewalks.

By the time Roy's mother returned, the garbage strike was over. Roy told her about the rats sitting in his fire truck and climbing up the wall and his grandmother swatting them with a broom. "Not all the rats are in Chicago, Roy," she said. "They got 'em in Minnesota, too."

"And in Venezuela," Roy started to say, but he didn't.

A Good Man to Know

I was seven years old in June of 1954 when my dad and I drove from Miami to New Orleans to visit his friend Albert Thibodeaux. It was a cloudy, humid morning when we rolled into town in my dad's powder-blue Cadillac. The river smell mixed with malt from the Jax brewery and the smoke from my dad's chain of Lucky Strikes to give the air an odor of toasted heat. We parked the car by Jackson Square and walked over a block to Tujague's bar to meet Albert. "It feels like it's going to rain," I said to Dad. "It always feels like this in New Orleans," he said.

Albert Thibodeaux was a gambler. In the evenings he presided over cockfight and pit-bull matches across the river in Gretna or Algiers but during the day he hung out at Tujague's on Decatur Street with the railroad men and phony artists from the Quarter. He and my dad knew each other from the old days in Cuba, which I knew nothing about except that they'd both lived at the Nacional in Havana.

According to Nanny, my mother's mother, my dad didn't even speak to me until I was five years old. He apparently didn't consider a child capable of understanding him or a friendship worth cultivating until that age and he may have been correct in his judgment. I certainly never felt deprived as a result of this policy. If my grandmother hadn't told me about it I would have never known the difference.

My dad never really told me about what he did or had done before I was old enough to go around with him. I picked up information as I went, listening to guys like Albert and some of my dad's other friends like Willie Nero in Chicago and Dummy Fish in New York. We supposedly lived in Chicago but my dad had places in Miami, New York, and Acapulco. We traveled, mostly without my mother, who stayed at the house in Chicago and went to church a lot. Once I asked my dad if we were any particular religion and he said, "Your mother's a Catholic."

Albert was a short, fat man with a handlebar mustache. He looked like a Maxwell Street organ-grinder without the organ or the monkey. He and my dad drank Irish whiskey from ten in the morning until lunchtime, which was around one-thirty, when they sent me down to the Central Grocery on Decatur or to Johnny's on St. Louis Street for muffaletas. I brought back three of them but Albert and Dad didn't eat theirs. They just talked and once in a while Albert went into the back to make a phone call. They got along just fine and about once an hour Albert would ask if I wanted something, like a Barq's or a Delaware Punch, and Dad would rub my shoulder and say to Albert, "He's a real piece of meat, this boy." Then Albert would grin so that his mustache covered the front of his nose and say, "He is, Rudy. You won't want to worry about him."

When Dad and I were in New York one night I heard him talking in a loud voice to Dummy Fish in the lobby of the Waldorf. I was sitting in a big leather chair between a sand-filled ashtray and a potted palm and Dad came over and told me that Dummy would take me upstairs to our room. I should go to sleep, he said, he'd be back late. In the elevator I looked at Dummy and saw that he was sweating. It was December but water ran down from his temples to his chin. "Does my dad have a job?" I asked Dummy. "Sure he does," he said. "Of course. Your dad has to work, just like everybody else." "What is it?" I asked. Dummy wiped the sweat from his face with a white-and-blue checkered handkerchief. "He talks to people," Dummy told me. "Your dad is a great talker."

Dad and Albert talked right past lunchtime and I must have fallen asleep on the bar because when I woke up it was dark out and I was in the backseat of the car. We were driving across the Huey P. Long Bridge and a freight train was running along the tracks over our heads. "How about some Italian oysters, son?" my dad asked. "We'll stop up here in Houma and get some cold beer and dinner." We were cruising in the passing lane in the powder blue Caddy over the big brown river. Through the bridge railings I watched the barge lights twinkle as they inched ahead through the water.

"Albert's a businessman, the best kind." Dad lit a fresh Lucky from an old one and threw the butt out the window. "He's a good man to know, remember that."

The Forgotten

It was snowing again and Roy couldn't wait to get out in it. Standing in line with the other second graders, all of them with their coats, mufflers, hats and gloves on, he was impatient to be released for morning recess. Roy had just told Eddie Gray that if the snow was deep enough they should choose up sides for a game of Plunge, when the teacher, Mrs. Bluth, called out to him.

"Roy! You know that you are not supposed to talk while I am giving instructions. You remain here while I take the rest of the class down to the playground."

Roy stood still while everyone else filed out of the classroom. As soon as he was sure that they were on their way down the west staircase, Roy walked out of the room and headed in the opposite direction. Nobody was in the hallway. Roy walked down the east staircase to the ground floor and through the exit to the street. Snow was coming down hard and Roy put up the hood of his dark blue parka as he headed north on Fairfield Avenue. He could hear the kids yelling in the playground on the other side of the school.

At the corner of Rosemont and Washtenaw, near St. Tim's, Roy passed an old man wearing a brown trenchcoat and a black hat who was holding a handdrawn sign that said, "I am a brother to dragons, and a companion to owls. JOB, 30:28."

"How old are you?" the man asked Roy.

"Seven," Roy answered, and kept walking.

"Read the Bible!" the man shouted. "Don't forget, like I did!"

When Roy entered the house, his mother was seated in front of the television set in the living room, drinking coffee.

"Is that you, Roy?" she asked. "I thought you were at school. It's only a little after ten."

"They let us out early today," he said. Roy went over to where she was sitting. "What's on?"

"*The Lady from Shanghai*. It's a good one. Rita Hayworth with her hair bleached blonde. Do you think I'd look as good as a blonde, Roy?"

"I don't know, Ma. I like you the way you are."

She kissed him on his forehead. Roy never drank coffee but he liked the odor of it.

"I'm going to play in my room," he said.

"Okay, honey."

About half an hour later, Roy heard the telephone ring and his mother answer it.

"Yes, this is she," she said into the receiver. "Uh huh, he is. He's in his room right now. Oh, really. I see. Yes, well, that will be between you and Roy, won't it? I'm sure he had a good reason. I understand. He'll be there tomorrow, yes. Thank you for calling."

Roy heard his mother hang up, then go into the kitchen and run water in the sink. A few minutes later, she appeared in the doorway to his room.

"Sweetheart," she said, "I have to go out for a little while. Is there anything you'd like me to pick up at the grocery store?"

"No, thanks, Ma."

"You'll be all right?"

"Sure, I'll be fine. I'm just playing with my soldiers."

"Which ones are those?" she asked.

"French Zouaves."

"Their uniforms are very beautiful. I've never seen soldiers with purple blouses before."

"These Zouaves are from Algeria," said Roy, "that's why their faces and hands are brown. They fought for France."

"And white turbans, too," his mother said. "Lana Turner wore one in *The Postman Always Rings Twice*. Do you remember that movie, Roy? Where she and John Garfield, who's a short order cook, kill her husband, who's much older than she is?"

"No, Ma, I don't."

"Thanks to a tricky lawyer, at first they get away with the murder, but then they slip up."

His mother stood there for a minute and watched Roy move the pretty Zouaves around the floor before saying, "I'm going now, honey. I'll be back in an hour."

"Okay, Ma."

"I'll make us grilled cheese sandwiches when I get back," she said, "and maybe some tomato soup."

It wasn't until after he heard the front door close that he took off his coat.

The next day at school, when he entered the classroom, Mrs. Bluth said, "Good morning, Roy. How are you feeling today?"

"Fine, Mrs. Bluth," he said, and took his seat.

The other kids looked at Roy but didn't say anything. Later, on the playground during morning recess, Eddie Gray asked Roy if he'd gotten into trouble for having left school without permission the day before.

"No," Roy said.

"Your mother didn't yell at you?"

"No."

"Why'd you leave?" Eddie asked.

"I didn't like the way Mrs. Bluth talked to me."

A few flurries began falling. Roy put up his hood.

"What about your dad?" asked Eddie. "What did he do?"

"My father's dead," said Roy.

"You're lucky," said Eddie Gray, "my old man would have used his belt on me."

Mrs. Kashfi

My mother has always been a great believer in fortune-tellers, a predilection my dad considered as bizarre as her devotion to the Catholic Church. He refused even to discuss anything having to do with either entity, a policy that seemed only to reinforce my mother's arcane quest. Even now she informs me whenever she's stumbled upon a seer whose prognostications strike her as being particularly apt. I once heard my dad describe her as belonging to "the sisterhood of the Perpetual Pursuit of the Good Word."

My own experience with fortune-tellers is limited to what I observed as a small boy, when I had no choice but to accompany my mother on her frequent pilgrimages to Mrs. Kashfi. Mrs. Kashfi was a tea-leaf reader who lived with her bird in a two-room apartment in a large gray brick building on Hollywood Avenue in Chicago. As soon as we entered the downstairs lobby the stuffiness of the place began to overwhelm me. It was as if Mrs. Kashfi lived in a vault to which no fresh air was admitted. The lobby, elevator, and hallways were suffocating, too hot both in summer, when there was too little ventilation, and in winter, when the building was unbearably overheated. And the whole place stank terribly, as if no food other than boiled cabbage were allowed to be prepared. My mother, who was usually all too aware of these sorts of unappealing aspects, seemed blissfully unaware of them at Mrs. Kashfi's. The oracle was in residence, and that was all that mattered.

The worst olfactory assault, however, came from Mrs. Kashfi's apartment, in the front room where her bird, a blind, practically featherless dinge-yellow parakeet, was kept and whose cage Mrs. Kashfi failed to clean with any regularity. It was in that room, on a lumpy couch with dirt-gray lace doily arm covers, that I was made to wait for my mother while she and Mrs. Kashfi, locked in the inner sanctum of the bedroom, voyaged into the sea of clairvoyance.

The apartment was filled with overstuffed chairs and couches, dressers crowded with bric-a-brac and framed photographs of strangely dressed, stiff and staring figures, relics of the old country, which to me appeared as evidence of extraterrestrial existence. Nothing seemed quite real, as if with a snap of Mrs. Kashfi's sorceress's fingers the entire scene would disappear. Mrs. Kashfi herself was a small, very old woman who was permanently bent slightly forwards so that she appeared about to topple over, causing me to avoid allowing her to hover over me for longer than a moment. She had a large nose and she wore glasses, as well as two or more dark green or brown sweaters at all times, despite the already hellish climate.

I dutifully sat on the couch, listening to the murmurings from beyond the bedroom door, and to the blind bird drop pelletlike feces onto the stained newspaper in its filthy cage. No sound issued from the parakeet's enclosure other than the constant "tup, tup" of its evacuation. Behind the birdcage was a weather-smeared window, covered with eyelet curtains, that looked out on the brick wall of another building.

I stayed put on the couch and waited for my mother's session to end. Each visit lasted about a half hour, at the finish of which Mrs. Kashfi would walk my mother to the doorway, where they'd stand and talk for another ten minutes while I fidgeted in the smelly hall trying to see how long I could hold my breath.

Only once did I have a glimpse of the mundane evidence from which Mrs. Kashfi made her miraculous analysis. At the conclusion of a session my mother came out of the bedroom carrying a teacup, which she told me to look into.

"What does it mean?" I asked.

"Your grandmother is safe and happy," my mother said.

My grandmother, my mother's mother, had recently died, so this news puzzled me. I looked again at the brown bits in the bottom of the china cup. Mrs. Kashfi came over and leaned above me, nodding her big nose with long hairs in the nostrils. I moved away and waited by the door, wondering what my dad would have thought of all this, while my mother stood smiling, staring into the cup.

The Old Country

My grandfather never wore an overcoat. That was Ezra, my father's father, who had a candy stand under the Addison Street elevated tracks near Wrigley Field. Even in winter, when it was ten below and the wind cut through the station, Ezra never wore more than a heavy sport coat, and sometimes, when Aunt Belle, his second wife, insisted, a woolen scarf wrapped up around his chin. He was six foot two and two hundred pounds, had his upper lip covered by a bushy mustache, and a full head of dark hair until he died at ninety, not missing a day at his stand till six months before.

He never told anyone his business. He ran numbers from the stand and owned an apartment building on the South Side. He outlived three wives and one of his sons, my father. His older son, my uncle Bruno, looked just like him, but Bruno was mean and defensive whereas Ezra was brusque but kind. He always gave me and my friends gum or candy on our way to and from the ballpark, and he liked me to hang around there or at another stand he had for a while at Belmont Avenue, especially on Saturdays so he could show me off to his regular cronies. He'd put me on a box behind the stand and keep one big hand on my shoulder. "This is my *grandson*," he'd say, and wait until he was sure they had looked at me. I was the first and then his only grandson; Uncle Bruno had two girls. "Good *boy!*"

He left it to his sons to make the big money, and they did all right, my dad with the rackets and the liquor store, Uncle Bruno as an auctioneer, but they never had to take care of the old man, he took care of himself.

Ezra spoke broken English; he came to America with his sons (my dad was eight, Bruno fourteen) and a daughter from Vienna in 1918. I always remember him standing under the tracks outside the station in February, cigar stub poked out between mustache and muffler, waiting for me and my dad to pick him up. When we'd pull up along the curb my dad would honk but the old man wouldn't notice. I would always have to run out and get him. I figured Ezra always saw us but waited for me to come for him. It made him feel better if I got out and grabbed his hand and led him to the car.

"Pa, for Chrissakes, why don't you wear an overcoat?" my dad would ask. "It's cold."

The old man wouldn't look over or answer right away. He'd sit with me on his lap as my father pointed the car into the dark.

"What cold?" he'd say after we'd gone a block or two. "In the *old* country was cold."

The Monster

I used to sit on a stool at the counter of the soda fountain in my dad's drugstore and talk to Louise, the counter waitress, while she made milk shakes and grilled cheese sandwiches. I especially liked to be there on Saturday mornings when the organ-grinder came in with his monkey. The monkey and I would dunk doughnuts together in the organ-grinder's coffee. The regular customers would always stop and say something to me, and tell my dad how much I looked like him, only handsomer.

One Saturday morning when I was about six, while I was waiting for the organ-grinder and his monkey to come in, I started talking to Louise about scary movies. I had seen *Frankenstein* the night before and I told Louise it was the scariest movie I'd ever seen, even scarier than *The Beast from 20,000 Fathoms* that my dad had taken me to see at the Oriental Theater when I was five. I had had dreams about the beast ripping up Coney Island and dropping big blobs of blood all over the streets ever since, but the part where the Frankenstein monster kills the little girl while she's picking flowers was worse than that.

"The scariest for me," Louise told me, "is *Dracula*. There'll never be another one like that."

I hadn't seen *Dracula* and I asked her what it was about.

Louise put on a new pot of coffee, then she turned and rested her arms on the counter in front of me.

"Sex, honey," she said. "Dracula was a vampire who went around attacking women. Oh, he might have attacked a man now and then, but he mainly went after the girls. Scared me to death when I saw it. I can't watch it now. I remember his eyes."

Then Louise went to take care of a customer. I stared at myself in the mirror behind the counter and thought about the little girl picking flowers with the monster.

The Ciné

On a cloudy October Saturday in 1953, when Roy was seven years old, his father took him to see a movie at the Ciné theater on Bukovina Avenue in Chicago, where they lived. Roy's father drove them in his powder-blue Cadillac, bumping over cobblestones and streetcar tracks, until he parked the car half a block away from the theater.

Roy was wearing a brown and white checked wool sweater, khaki trousers and saddle shoes. His father wore a double-breasted blue suit with a white silk tie. They held hands as they walked toward the Ciné. The air was becoming colder every day now, Roy noticed, and he was eager to get inside the theater, to be away from the wind. The Ciné sign had a red background over which the letters curved vertically in yellow neon. They snaked into one another like reticulate pythons threaded through branches of a thick-trunked Cambodian bo tree. The marquee advertised the movie they were going to see, *King of the Khyber Rifles*, starring Tyrone Power as King, a half-caste British officer commanding Indian cavalry riding against Afghan and other insurgents. "Tyrone Cupcake," Roy's father called him, but Roy did not know why.

Roy and his father entered the Ciné lobby and headed for the concession stand, where Roy's father bought Roy buttered popcorn, a Holloway All-Day sucker and a Dad's root beer. Inside the cinema, they chose seats fairly close to the screen on the right-hand side. The audience was composed mostly of kids, many of whom ran up and down the aisles even during the show, shouting and laughing, falling and spilling popcorn and drinks.

The movie began soon after Roy and his father were in their seats, and as Tyrone Power was reviewing his mounted troops, Roy's father whispered to his son, "The Afghans were making money off the opium trade even back then."

"What's opium, Dad?" asked Roy.

"Hop made from poppies. The Afghans grow and sell them to dope dealers in other countries. Opium makes people very sick."

"Do people eat it?"

"They can, but mostly they smoke it and dream."

"Do they have bad dreams?"

"Probably bad and good. Users get ga-ga on the pipe. Once somebody's hooked on O, he's finished as a man."

"What about women? Do they smoke it, too?"

"Sure, son. Only Orientals, though, that I know of. Sailors in Shanghai, Hong Kong, Zamboanga, get on the stem and never make it back to civilization."

"Where's Zamboanga?"

"On Mindanao, in the Philippine Islands."

"Is that a long way from India and Afghanistan?"

"Every place out there is a long way from everywhere else."

"Can't the Khyber Rifles stop the Afghans?"

"Tyrone Cupcake'll kick 'em in the pants if they don't."

Roy and his father watched Tyrone Power wrangle his

minions for about twenty minutes before Roy's father whispered in Roy's ear again.

"Son, I've got to take care of something. I'll be back in a little while. Before the movie's over. Here's a dollar," he said, sticking a bill into Roy's hand, "just in case you want more popcorn."

"Dad," said Roy, "don't you want to see what happens?"

"You'll tell me later. Enjoy the movie, son. Wait for me here."

Before Roy could say anything else, his father was gone. The movie ended and Roy's father had not returned. Roy remained in his seat while the lights were on. He had eaten the popcorn and drunk his root beer but he had not yet unwrapped the Holloway All-Day sucker. People left the theater and other people came in and took their seats. The movie began again.

Roy had to pee badly but he did not want to leave his seat in case his father came back while he was in the men's room. Roy held it until he could not any longer and then allowed a ribbon of urine to trickle down his left pantsleg into his sock and onto the floor. The chair on his left, where his father had been sitting, was empty, and an old lady seated on his right did not seem to notice that Roy had urinated. The odor was covered up by the smells of popcorn, candy and cigarettes.

Roy sat in his wet trousers and soaked left sock and shoe, watching again as Captain King exhorted his Khyber Rifles to perform heroically. This time after the film was finished Roy got up and walked out with the rest of the audience. He stood under the theater marquee and waited for his father. It felt good to be out of the close, smoky cinema now. The sky was dark, just past dusk, and the people filing in the Ciné were mostly couples on Saturday night dates.

Roy was getting hungry. He took out the Holloway all-Day, unwrapped it and took a lick. A uniformed policeman came and stood near him. Roy was not tempted to say anything about his situation to the beat cop because he remembered his father saying to him more than once, "The police are not your friends." The police officer looked once at Roy, smiled at him, then moved away.

Roy's mother was in Cincinnati, visiting her sister, Roy's aunt Theresa. Roy decided to walk to where his father had parked, to see if his powder-blue Cadillac was still there. Maybe his father had gone wherever he had gone on foot, or taken a taxi. A black and gold-trimmed Studebaker Hawk was parked where Roy's father's car had been.

Roy returned to the Ciné. The policeman who had smiled at him was standing again in front of the theater. Roy passed by without looking at the cop, licking his Holloway All-Day. His left pantsleg felt crusty but almost dry and his sock still felt soggy. The cold wind made Roy shiver and he rubbed his arms. A car horn honked. Roy turned and saw the powder-blue Caddy stopped in the street. His father was waving at him out the driver's side window.

Roy walked to and around the front of the car, opened the passenger side door and climbed in, pulling the heavy metal door closed. Roy's father started driving. Roy looked out the window at the cop standing in front of the Ciné: one of his hands rested on the butt of his holstered pistol and the other fingered grooves on the handle of his billy club as his eyes swept the street.

"Sorry I'm late, son," Roy's father said, "Took me a little longer than I thought it would. Happens sometimes. How was the movie? Did Ty Cupcake take care of business?"

Dark Mink

Pops, my other grandfather, my mother's father, and his brothers spent much of their time playing bridge and talking baseball in the back room of their fur coat business. From the time I was four or five Pops would set me up on a high stool at a counter under a window looking down on State Street and give me a furrier's knife with a few small pelts to cut up. I spent whole afternoons that way, wearing a much-too-large-for-me apron with the tie strings wrapped several times around my waist, cutting up mink, beaver, fox, squirrel, even occasional leopard or seal squares, careful not to slice my finger with the razor-sharp mole-shaped tool, while the wet snow slid down the high, filthy State and Lake Building windows and Pops and my great-uncles Ike, Nate, and Louie played cards.

They were all great baseball fans, they were gentlemen, and didn't care much for other sports, so even in winter the card table tended to be hot-stove league speculation about off-season trades or whether or not Sauer's legs would hold up for another season. Of course there were times customers came in, well-to-do women with their financier husbands, looking as if they'd stepped out of a Peter Arno *New Yorker* cartoon; or gangsters with their girlfriends, heavy-overcoated guys with thick cigars wedged between leather-gloved fingers. I watched the women model the coats and straighten their stocking seams in the four-sided full-length mirrors. I liked dark mink the best, those ankle-length, full-collar, silk-lined ones that smelled so good with leftover traces of perfume. There was no more luxurious feeling than to nap under my mother's own sixty-pelt coat.

By the time the fur business bottomed out, Pops was several years dead—he'd lived to eighty-two—and so was Uncle Ike, at eighty-eight. Pops had seen all of the old-time great ballplayers, Tris Speaker, the Babe, even Joe Jackson, who he said was the greatest player of them all. When the White Sox clinched the American League pennant in 1959, the first flag for them in forty years (since the Black Sox scandal of 1919), he and I watched the game on television. The Sox were playing Cleveland, and to end it the Sox turned over one of their 141 double plays of that season, Aparicio to Fox to Big Ted Kluszewski.

Uncle Nate and Uncle Louie kept on for some time, going in to work each day not as furriers but to Uncle Louie's Chicago Furriers Association office. He'd founded the association in the '20s, acting as representative to the Chamber of Commerce, Better Business Bureau, and other civic organizations. Louie was also a poet. He'd written verse, he told me, in every form imaginable. Most of them he showed me were occasional poems, written to celebrate coronations—the brothers had all been born and raised in London—and inaugurations of American presidents. In the middle right-hand drawer of his desk he kept boxes of Dutch-shoe chocolates, which he would give me whenever I came to visit him.

Uncle Nate, who lived to be 102, came in to Uncle Louie's office clean-shaven and with an impeccable high-starched collar every day until he was a hundred. He once told me he knew he would live that long because of a prophecy by an old man in a wheelchair he'd helped cross a London street when he was seven. The man had put his hand on Nate's head, blessed him, and told him he'd live a century.

Uncle Louie was the last to go, at ninety-four. Having long since moved away, I didn't find out about his death until a year or so later. The fur business, as my grandfather and his brothers had known it, was long gone; even the State and Lake Building was about to be torn down, a fate that had already befallen Fritzl's, where the brothers had gone each day for lunch. Fritzl's had been the premier restaurant of the Loop in those days, with large leather booths, big white linen napkins, and thick, high-stemmed glasses. Like the old Lindy's in New York, Fritzl's was frequented by show people, entertainers, including ballplayers, and newspaper columnists. Many of the women who had bought coats, or had had coats bought for them, at my grandfather's place, ate there. I was always pleased to recognize one of them, drinking a martini or picking at a shrimp salad, the fabulous dark mink draped gracefully nearby.

Nanny

From the time I was four until I was eight my grandmother lived with us. She slept in the big bedroom with my mother (my father had remarried by then) and was bedridden most of the time, her heart condition critical, killing her just past her sixtieth birthday. I called her Nanny, for no reason I can remember, and I loved her, as small boys suppose they do. My mother was often away in those days, and while I don't remember Nanny ever feeding me (too sick to get out of bed for that) or dressing me, or making me laugh (there was Flo for that, my black mammy who later "ran off with some man," as my mother was wont to disclose; and then a succession of other maids and nurses most of whom, again according to my mother, either ransacked liquor cabinets or ran away à la Flo—anyone who left my mother always "ran off"), I do remember her scolding me, and once my mother was in Puerto Rico, for some reason I'm sure Nanny considered adequate (sufficient to pry her from bed), she backed me into a corner of my room against the full-length mirror on my closet door (thus I watched her though my back was turned) and beat me with a board, me screaming, "My mother'll get you for this!"; and when my mother returned my not believing it was really her (she being so brown from the sun), and my momentary fear of her being an impostor, some woman hired by my grandmother to beat me because it was too hard on her heart for her to do it herself.

This repeated paranoia, persistent tension, allowed no relief for me then but through my toy soldiers, sworded dragoons, Zouaves, and Vikings that I manipulated, controlled. Hours alone on my lined linoleum floor I played, determinedly oblivious to the voices, agonies perpetuated dining room to kitchen to bedroom.

And there was the race we never ran. Nanny and I planned a race for when she was well, though she never would be. Days sick I'd sit in my mother's bed next to Nanny and devise the route, from backyard down the block to the corner, from the fence to the lamppost and back—and Nanny would nod, "Yes, certainly, soon as I'm well"—and I'd cut out comics or draw, listening to Sergeant Preston on the radio, running the race in my mind, running it over and over, never once seeing Nanny run with me.

Island in the Sun

"**O**h, Roy, this poor thing!"

"Who, Mom? What poor thing?"

Roy was eating breakfast in their room at the Casa Marina in Key West, Corn Flakes with milk and red banana slices on it. His mother had a cup of Cuban coffee and a small glass of freshly squeezed orange juice on the table in front of her. She was reading the *Miami Herald*.

"This sick man in a big city up north who was beaten to death by teenagers. How terrible."

Roy looked out through the open French doors to the terrace and beyond to the Atlantic Ocean. The water was very blue and he knew it would be cold despite the bright December sun. If they decided to swim today, Roy thought, he and his mother would go to the other side of the island and swim in the Gulf of Mexico, where the water was always warmer.

"Why would they beat up a sick man?"

"He was mentally retarded and weighed 300 pounds and wore a homemade Batman costume. The neighborhood kids liked to pick on him and call him names."

"What was his real name?"

"Jimmy Rodriguez."

"How old was he?"

"Forty-two. Listen, Roy: 'Mr. Rodriguez lived alone in the

city's most crime-ridden district. Neighbors told police that he would often shout at drug dealers and prostitutes from the sidewalk outside the apartment building in which he lived.'"

"Does it tell about how it happened?"

"'Two fourteen year old boys and one thirteen year old girl hit him with soda pop bottles until he fell. Then they kicked him and poured soda on him while they shouted, 'Fatman not Batman! Fatman not Batman!'"

"Even the girl?"

"Mm-hm. The kids kept beating and kicking him even after he was dead, a neighbor, Feliciana Domingo, told police. Oh, Roy, this is really sad."

"What, Mom?"

"Batman had bought the bottles of soda pop for the kids who killed him."

Roy had never lived in a real neighborhood. He was eight years old and had grown up in hotels. His mother put down the newspaper, picked up her cup and took a sip of coffee.

"What happened to the kids who did it?"

"I don't know, it doesn't say. They'll probably be sent to a reformatory."

Roy's mother put down her cup, lit a Pall Mall, inhaled deeply, then blew the smoke toward the terrace. White curlicues floated in the air for a few seconds in front of the dark blue water, then vanished.

"What does retarded mean?"

"Slow, Roy. Batman's brain didn't work fast."

"Mom, I'm full."

"Okay, baby, don't eat any more. As soon as I finish my cigarette, we'll go to the beach."

"Probably Batman never went to a beach."

Roy's mother puffed and turned halfway around in her chair to stare at the ocean.

"Why did he live alone? Somebody should have taken care of him."

"Yes, Roy, somebody should have. The poor thing."

Roy watched a horsefly land on one of the sugar cubes that were crowded in a small green bowl next to his mother's cup and saucer. He remembered his father once saying that he knew a guy named Art Huck who would bet on anything, even which cube of sugar a fly would land on.

"Mom, do you know a man named Art Huck?"

"No, I don't think so. Who is he?"

"A friend of Dad's."

His mother sat still, looking toward the water.

"What are you thinking about?"

"I'm not sure which is worse, Roy, an act of cruelty or an act of cowardice."

"Maybe they're the same."

"No, actually I think cruelty is worse, because it's premeditated."

"What's that mean?"

"You have to think about it before you do it."

"You're always telling me to think before I do something."

"You're not a cruel person, Roy. You never will be."

"Do you know any cruel people?"

Roy's mother stood up and walked out onto the terrace. She threw her cigarette away.

"Yes, Roy," she said, without turning to look at him, "unfortunately, I do."

An Eye on the Alligators

I knew as the boat pulled in to the dock there were no alligators out there. I got up and stuck my foot against the piling so that it wouldn't scrape the boat, then got out and secured the bowline to the nearest cleat. Mr. Reed was standing on the dock now, helping my mother up out of the boat. Her brown legs came up off the edge weakly, so that Mr. Reed had to lift her to keep her from falling back. The water by the pier was blue black and stank of oil and gas, not like out on the ocean, or in the channel, where we had been that day.

Mr. Reed had told me to watch for the alligators. The best spot to do it from, he said, was up on the bow. So I crawled up through the trapdoor on the bow and watched for the alligators. The river water was clear and green.

"Look around the rocks," Mr. Reed shouted over the engine noise, "the gators like the rocks." So I kept my eye on the rocks, but there were no alligators.

"I don't see any," I shouted. "Maybe we're going too fast and the noise scares them away."

After that Mr. Reed went slower but still there were no alligators. We were out for nearly three hours and I didn't see one.

"It was just a bad day for seeing alligators, son," said Mr.

Reed. "Probably because of the rain. They don't like to come up when it's raining."

For some reason I didn't like it when Mr. Reed called me "son." I wasn't his son. Mr. Reed, my mother told me, was a friend of my father's. My dad was not in Florida with us, he was in Chicago doing business while my mother and I rode around in boats and visited alligator farms.

Mr. Reed had one arm around me and one arm around my mother.

"Can we go back tomorrow?" I asked.

My mother laughed. "That's up to Mr. Reed," she said. "We don't want to impose on him too much."

"Sure kid," said Mr. Reed. Then he laughed, too.

I looked up at Mr. Reed, then out at the water. I could see the drops disappearing into their holes on the surface.

The Piano Lesson

I bounced the ball against the yellow wall in the front of my house, waiting for the piano teacher. I'd been taking lessons for six weeks and I liked the piano, my mother played well, standards and show tunes, and sang. Often I sang along with her or by myself as she played. "Young at Heart" and "Bewitched, Bothered and Bewildered" were two of my favorites. I loved the dark blue cover of the sheet music of "Bewitched," with the drawing of the woman in a flowing white gown in the lower left-hand corner. It made me think of New York, though I'd never been there. White on midnight dark.

I liked to stand next to the piano bench while my mother played and listen to "Satan Takes a Holiday," a fox-trot it said on the sheet music. I was eight years old and could easily imagine foxes trotting in evening gowns.

I was up to "The Scissors-Grinder" and "Swan on the Lake" in the second red Thompson book. That was pretty good for six weeks, but I had begun to stutter. I knew I had begun to stutter because I'd heard my mother say it to my father on the phone. They ought just to ignore it, she'd said, and it would stop.

"Ready for your lesson today?" asked the teacher as she came up the walk.

"I'll be in in a minute," I said, continuing to bounce the ball off the yellow bricks. The teacher smiled and went into the building.

I kept hitting the ball against the wall. I knew she would be talking to my mother, then arranging the lesson books on the rack above the piano. I hit the ball once high above the first-floor windows, caught it, and ran.

The Lost Tribe

Roy looked for the tall black man whenever he walked past the yellow brick synagogue on his way to his friend Elmo's house. The man always waved to Roy and Roy waved back but they had never spoken. The man was usually sweeping the synagogue steps with a broom or emptying small trash cans into bigger ones. Seeing a black man working as a janitor was not an unusual sight, but what was unusual, to Roy, was that the man always wore a yarmulke. Roy had never before seen a black person wearing a Jewish prayer cap. Elmo was Jewish, so Roy asked him if anybody could be a Jew, even a black man.

"I don't know," said Elmo. "Maybe. Let's ask my old man."

Elmo's father, Big Sol, was a short but powerfully built man who owned a salvage business on the south side of Chicago. When Big Sol was home, he usually wore a Polish T-shirt, white boxer shorts, black socks and fuzzy house slippers. He was very hairy; large tufts of hair puffed out all over his body except for from the top of his head, which was bald. Big Sol was a kind, generous man who enjoyed joking around with the neighborhood kids, to whom he frequently offered a buck or two for soda pop or ice cream.

Big Sol was sitting in his recliner watching television when Elmo and Roy approached him.

"Hey, boys, how you doin'? Come on in, I'm watchin' a movie."

Roy looked at the black and white picture. James Mason was being chased by several men on a dark, wet street.

"This James Mason," said Big Sol, "he talks like he's got too many meatballs in his mouth."

Roy remembered Elmo having told him his father had been wounded at Guadalcanal. He'd recovered and was sent back into combat but later contracted malaria, which got him medically discharged from the Marines. Elmo was named after a war buddy of Big Sol's who had not been as fortunate.

"Hey, Pop," Elmo said, "can anybody be a Jew?"

"This is America," said Big Sol. "A person can be anything he wants to be. "

"How about Negroes?" said Elmo. "Can a Negro be Jewish?"

"Sammy Davis, Junior, is a Jew," Big Sol said.

"Was he born a Jew?" Elmo asked.

"What difference does it make? Sammy Davis, Junior, is the greatest entertainer in the world."

A few days later, Roy was walking past the synagogue thinking about how he had never been inside one, when he saw the black janitor wringing out a mop by the back door. The man waved and smiled. Roy went over to him.

"What's your name?" asked Roy.

"Ezra. What's yours?"

"Roy."

Ezra offered his right hand and Roy offered his. As they shook, Roy was surprised at how rough Ezra's skin was; almost abrasive, like a shark's.

"How old are you, Roy?"

"Eight. How old are you?"

"Sixty-one next Tuesday."

"How come you're wearing a Jewish prayer hat?" Roy asked.

"You got to wear one in the temple," said Ezra. "It's a holy place."

"Are you a Jew?"

"I am now."

"You weren't always?"

"Son, that's a good question. I was but I didn't know it until late in my life."

"How come?"

"Never really understood the Bible before, Roy. The original Jews were black, in Africa. I'm a descendant of the Lost Tribe of Israel."

"I've never heard of the Lost Tribe."

"You heard of Hailie Selassie?"

"No, who is he?"

"Hailie Selassie is the Lion of Judah. He lives in Ethiopia. Used to be called Abyssinia."

"Have you ever been there?"

Ezra shook his head. "Hope to go before I expire, though."

"How did your tribe get lost?"

"Old Pharaoh forced us to wander in the desert for thousands of years. Didn't want no Jews in Egypt. Drew down on us with six hundred chariots, but we got away when the angel of God put a pillar of cloud in front of 'em just long enough so Moses could herd us across the Red Sea, which the Lord divided then closed back up."

"Why didn't Pharaoh want the Jews in Egypt?"

Ezra bent down, looked Roy right in his eyes and said, "The Jews are the smartest people on the face of the earth.

Always have been, always will be. Old Pharaoh got frightened. Hitler, too."

Roy noticed that the whites of Ezra's eyes were not white; they were mostly yellow.

"They were scared of the Jews?"

Ezra straightened back up to his full height.

"You bet they were scared," he said. "People get scared, they commence to killin'. After awhile, they get used to it, same as eatin'."

Ezra picked up his mop and bucket.

"Nice talkin' to you, Roy. You stop by again."

Ezra turned and entered the synagogue.

Walking to Elmo's house, Roy thought about Ezra's tribe wandering lost in the desert. They must have been smart, Roy decided, to have survived for so long.

Big Sol was sitting in his easy chair in the living room, drinking a Falstaff and watching the White Sox play the Tigers on TV.

"Hey, Big Roy!" he said. "How you doin'?"

"Did the Lost Tribe of Israel really wander in the desert for thousands of years?" Roy asked.

Big Sol nodded his head. "Yeah, but that was a long time ago. The Jews were tough in them days."

"Ezra, the janitor at the synagogue up the street, told me that Jews are the smartest people on the planet."

Big Sol stared seriously at the TV for several seconds. Pierce struck Kaline out on a change-up.

"Yeah, well," Big Sol said, turning to look at Roy, "he won't get no argument from me."

The Lost Christmas

In 1954, when I was eight years old, I lost Christmas. At about noon of Christmas Eve that year, I went with some kids to the Nortown Theater on Western Avenue in Chicago to see a movie, *Demetrius and the Gladiators*, starring Victor Mature and Susan Hayward. My mother and I had until earlier that month been living in Florida and Cuba, and were in Chicago, where I was born and where we sometimes stayed, to spend the Christmas holidays with Nanny, my grandmother, my mother's mother, who was bed-ridden because of a chronic heart condition. In fact, Nanny would die due to heart failure the following May, at the age of fifty-nine.

The ground was piled with fresh snow that Christmas Eve Day. The few cars that were moving snailed along the streets barely faster than we could walk. The first time I had come to Chicago as a human being old enough to be conscious of my surroundings was when I was five or six. Now that I was older, however, and was somewhat inured to the snow and ice—at least I knew what to expect—I could if not enjoy at least endure the weather, especially since I knew my situation was temporary.

I thought *Demetrius and the Gladiators* was a great movie, full of fighting with swords and shields and a sexy redhead, like my mother. I didn't notice if Victor Mature's breasts were larger than Susan Hayward's—an earlier (1949) film, *Samson and Delilah,* had prompted the comment by a producer that Mature's tits were bigger than co-star Hedy Lamarr's—I was impressed only by the pageantry of goofy Hollywood ancient Rome. Walking home Christmas Eve afternoon, the leaden gray Chicago sky heading rapidly toward darkness, I suddenly was overcome by dizziness and very nearly collapsed to the now ice-hard sidewalk carapace. My companions had already turned off onto another street, so I was alone. I managed to steady myself against a brown brick wall and then slowly and carefully made my way the final block or two to my grandmother's house.

The next thing I knew I was waking up in bed dressed in my yellow flannel pajamas decorated with drawings of football players. The first image I saw was a large-jawed fullback cradling a ball in the crook of his left arm while stiff-arming a would-be tackler with his right. I was very thirsty and looked up to see my mother and Nanny, who, miraculously, was out of her sickbed, leaning over me. According to my mother, I asked two questions: "Can I have a glass of water?" and "Is it Christmas yet?"

In fact, it was December 26th—I had lost consciousness almost as soon as I arrived home following the movie, and had been delirious with fever for most of the time since then. The fever broke and I woke up. My mother brought me a glass of water, which she cautioned me to sip slowly, as the doctor had ordered.

"Was the doctor here?" I asked. Nanny and my mother told me how worried they had been. A doctor friend of Nanny's had come twice to see me, even on Christmas Day; he would come again later. Nanny and my mother laughed—in fact, both of them were crying tears of relief.

"This is the best gift of all," said my mother, "getting my boy back."

I've often wondered what I missed during my delirium, as if those twenty-four or so hours had been stolen from me. Once someone asked me if I had access to a time machine and could go forward or back anywhere in time, where would I go? I told him without hesitation that I would set the machine for Christmas Day of 1954. To paraphrase William Faulkner, that Christmas past is not dead, it's not even past.

My Catechism

It was during the winter I later referred to, in deference to the poet, as Out of the Clouds Endlessly Snowing, that I was dismissed once and forever from Sunday school. Mine was not a consistent presence at St. Tim's, due to my mother's predilection for travel and preference for tropical places, but the winter after I turned eight years old, she left me for several weeks with her mother, whom I called Nanny, in Chicago. Where exactly my mother chose to spend that period of time I've never been entirely certain, although I believe she was then keeping company—my mother and father were divorced—with a gunrunner of Syrian or Lebanese descent named Johnny Cacao, whose main residence seemed to be in the Dominican Republic.

I recall receiving a soggy postcard postmarked Santo Domingo, on which my mother had written, "Big turtle bit off part of one of Johnny's toes. Other than that, doing fine. Sea green and crystal clear. Love, Mom." The picture side of the card showed a yellowish dirt street with a half-naked brown boy about my age sitting on the ground leaning against a darker brown wall. A pair of red chickens were pecking in the dust next to his bare feet. I wondered if the chickens down there went for toes the way the turtles did.

On this blizzardy Sunday morning, I walked to St. Tim's

with two of the three McLaughlin brothers, Petie and Paulie, and their mother. My mother and grandmother were Catholics but they rarely attended church; Nanny because she was most often too ill—she died before my ninth birthday—and my mother because she was so frequently away, swimming in turtle-infested seas. Petie and I were the same age, Paulie a year younger. The eldest McLaughlin brother, Frank, was in the Army, stationed in Korea.

After the church service, which was the first great theater I ever attended, and which I still rank as the best because the audience was always invited to participate by taking the wafer and the wine, symbolizing the body and the blood of Jesus Christ, Petie, Paulie and I went to catechism class. Ruled over by Sister Margaret Mary, a tall, sturdily built woman of indeterminate age—I could never figure out if she was twenty-five or fifty-five—the children sat ramrod straight in their chairs and did not speak unless invited to by her. Sister Margaret Mary wore a classic black habit, wire-rimmed spectacles, and her facial skin was as pale as one of Dracula's wives. I had recently seen the Tod Browning film, *Dracula*, featuring Bela Lugosi, and I remember thinking that it was interesting that both God and Dracula had similar taste in women.

During instruction, the class was given the standard mumbo jumbo, as my father—who was not a Catholic—called it, about how God created heaven and earth, then Adam and Eve, and so on. Kids asked how He had done this or that, and what He did next. I raised my hand and asked, "Sister, *why* did He do it?"

"Why did He do what?" she said.

"Any of this stuff."

"You wouldn't exist, or Peter or Paul, or His only son, had He not made us," answered Sister Margaret Mary.

"I know, Sister," I said, "but what for? I mean, what was in it for Him."

Sister Margaret Mary glared at me for a long moment, and for the first and only time I could discern a trace of color in her face. She then turned her attention away from me and proceeded as if my question deserved no further response.

Before we left the church that day, I saw Sister Margaret Mary talking to Mrs. McLaughlin and looking toward me as she spoke. Mrs. McLaughlin nodded, and looked over at me, too.

The following Sunday morning, I was about to leave the house when Nanny asked me where I was going.

"To the McLaughlins'," I told her. "To Sunday School."

"Sister Margaret Mary told Mrs. McLaughlin she doesn't want you coming to her class anymore," said Nanny. "You can play in your room or watch television until Petie and Paulie come home. Besides, it's snowing again."

Sunday Paper

As he often did when I was about eight or nine and he still lived with us, Pops, my mother's father, asked me to go for the Sunday paper. For some reason on this particular day I decided to go to the stand on Washtenaw instead of the one on Rockwell, taking the shortcut through the alley where the deep snow from the night before was still undisturbed, no cars having gone over it yet that morning. I was shuffling through the powder, kicking it up in the air so that the flakes floated about in the sunlight like rice snow in crystal balls, when I spotted the police cars.

There were three of them, parked one behind the other on Washtenaw in front of Talon's Butcher Shop. A few people stood bundled in coats outside Talon's, trying to see inside the shop, which I knew was closed on Sunday. I stood on the opposite side of the street and watched. An ambulance came, without using its siren, and slid slowly to a stop alongside the police cars. Two attendants got out and went into Talon's carrying a stretcher.

A man came up beside me and asked what was going on. I looked at him and saw that he had on an overcoat over his pajamas and probably slippers on under his galoshes.

"I was just going for a paper," he said.

When I told him I didn't know, he crossed over and spoke

to one of the women standing by the door of the butcher shop. The man looked in the doorway and then walked away. I waited, standing in a warm shaft of sunlight, and in a couple of minutes the man came up to me again. He had a rolled-up *Tribune* under his arm.

"He hanged himself," the man said. "Talon, the butcher. They found him hanging in his shop this morning."

The man looked across the street for a moment, then walked down Washtenaw.

Nobody came out of the butcher shop. I went to the corner and bought a *Sun-Times*. I stopped for a few seconds on my way back to see if anything was happening but nothing was so I turned into the alley, carefully stepping in the tracks I'd made before.

The Origin of Truth

When Roy was in the fourth grade, his class was taken on a field trip to the Museum of Science and Industry. Aboard the school bus on the way to the museum, Bobby Kazmeier and Jimmy Portis both said they couldn't wait to go down into the coal mine.

"They got a real working coal mine there," Portis told Roy and Big Art Tuth, Roy's seatmate, "like in West Virginia, where my daddy's family's from."

"It ain't real," said Big Art, "it's a reenactment."

"Not a reenactment," Roy said, "a reproduction, or a replica. It's to show what a coal mine is like."

"What's the difference?" asked Kazmeier. I heard you go down a mine shaft in an elevator."

"An open air one, Kaz," said Portis, "not like an elevator in the Wrigley Building."

"They've got open ones in the State and Lake Building," Roy said, "to deliver furs. My grandfather works there. Also in the Merchandise Mart. They're in the back; customers take the regular elevators."

"I hope we don't have to squeeze through any narrow places in the caves," said Big Art. "I don't want to get stuck."

Delbert Swaim, the dumbest kid in the class, who was sitting behind Roy, said, "I bet it's like in Flash Gordon, where the clay people blend into the walls and attack when nobody's looking."

In the museum, the class looked at outer space exhibits and architectural displays, which were pretty interesting, but the boys were anxious to go down into the coal mine. This was left for last. The class teacher, Mrs. Rudinsky, instructed the students to keep together.

"We'll descend in groups of ten," she announced. "That means three groups. When you reach the bottom, stay right there with your group until the others arrive. I will be with the third group."

Mrs. Rudinsky was not quite five feet tall, she was very skinny and wore thick glasses and a big black wig. She was forty-five years old. The story was that she had lost all of her hair as a teenager due to an attack of scarlet fever. Roy didn't know what scarlet fever was, so he asked Mary Margaret Grubart, the smartest girl in the class, about it.

"Fevers come in all colors," she told Roy. "Scarlet's one of the worst, it can kill a person. A man wrote a famous novel about it where a girl had to wear a scarlet letter on her dress to warn people not to get near her so they wouldn't get sick. In historical times, sick people were burned alive."

In the coal mine, the kids were shown around by a museum guide wearing a hard hat with a flashlight attached to the front of it, the kind that miners wear. There were blue flames that indicated gas deposits and a miniature railway on which carts carrying coal traveled. The guide explained how the operation worked and presented samples of different types of coal, which the students passed around. The hardest, blackest coal was called bituminous.

"This is the kind Superman can squeeze and turn into diamonds," said Roy.

The other kids laughed but the guide said, "You're right, son. Bituminous is processed over a period of hundreds if not thousands of years and can become diamonds."

"Superman can make a diamond in a few seconds," Roy said. "But he doesn't do it too often in order not to destroy the world economy. My grandfather told me that."

"Your grandfather knows what he's talking about, young man," said the guide.

After the tour had concluded and they were back above ground, Mrs. Rudinsky lined the students up preparatory to marching them out of the museum to the bus. Two boys were missing: Bobby Kazmeier and Jimmy Portis.

"Has anyone seen Portis and Kazmeier?" asked Mrs. Rudinsky.

"They're still down in the mine," said Delbert Swaim. "They said they wanted to explore more."

"You all wait right here!" Mrs. Rudinsky commanded, before going to find a museum employee.

While two security guards and the coal mine guide went down in the elevator to find the missing boys, Mrs. Rudinsky loaded the other students onto the school bus, where they were told to wait with the driver, Old Ed Moot. Mrs. Rudinsky went back into the museum.

"They could suffocate," said Old Ed Moot, "if they stay down there too long without masks."

It was more than an hour before Mrs. Rudinsky returned to the bus. Bobby Kazmeier and Jimmy Portis were not with her.

"Go!" she said to Old Ed Moot, and sat down in a seat at the front. Old Ed pulled the door closed.

"Mrs. Rudinsky, some of us have to go to the bathroom," said Mary Margaret Grubart.

"You'll just have to hold it until we get to the school," Mrs. Rudinsky told her.

"Where's Kaz and Jimmy?" asked Roy.

"They'll find them," the teacher said.

"You mean they're still down in the mine?" asked Big Art.

"No talking!" ordered Mrs. Rudinsky.

Roy noticed that her wig was turned slightly sideways and listing to port. Above her right ear, Mrs. Rudinsky's scalp was hairless.

She was the first person off the bus and headed straight for the principal's office, leaving the students to fend for themselves. The school day was over, everyone was free to go home, but Roy and Big Art stood by the bus with Old Ed Moot, who lit up an unfiltered Chesterfield.

"Those boys are in big trouble," said Old Ed, "unless they're dead. Either way, your teacher's in deep shit."

"Hey, Ed," said Big Art, "can we have a cigarette?"

Old Ed shook his head as he inhaled his Chesterfield. "Dirty habit," he said. "Don't start."

"We already started," said Art.

Just then a police car pulled up in front of the school. Two cops got out with Jimmy Portis between them and entered the building.

"Wow," Roy said, "where's Kaz?"

"Maybe suffocated," said the bus driver. "This one's the lucky one."

Two minutes later, another police car arrived and parked behind the first one. Two cops got out with Bobby Kazmeier wedged between them and walked into the school.

Old Ed Moot looked at the Timex on his left wrist and said, "Well, fellas, my day's done."

He dropped his cigarette butt on the ground and stepped on it, turning his steel-toed Sears workshoe so that there wouldn't be anything worth picking up, and walked away.

"What do you think will happen to them?" asked Big Art.

"I don't know," Roy said, "but if it hadn't been for Jimmy and Kaz staying in the coal mine, we probably would have got homework."

The Trophy

My dad was not much of an athlete. I don't recall his ever playing catch with me or doing anything requiring particular athletic dexterity. I knew he was a kind of tough guy because my mother told me about his knocking other guys down now and again, but he wasn't interested in sports. He did, however, take me to professional baseball and football games and boxing matches but those were, for him, more like social occasions, opportunities to meet and be greeted by business associates and potential customers. At Marigold Arena or the Amphitheater Dad spent most of his time talking to people rather than watching the event. He may have gone bowling on occasion but never in my company.

When I was nine I joined a winter bowling league. I was among the youngest bowlers in the league and certainly the youngest on my team. The league met on Saturday mornings at Nortown Bowl on Devon Avenue between Maplewood and Campbell Streets. The lanes were on the second floor up a long, decrepit flight of stairs above Crawford's Department Store. I told my dad about it and invited him to come watch me bowl. I wasn't very good, of course, but I took it seriously, as I did all competitive sports, and I steadily improved. I practiced after school a couple of times during the week with older guys, who gave me tips on how to improve my bowling skills.

There were kids who practically lived at the bowling alley. Most of them were sixteen or older and had pretty much given up on formal education. The state law in Illinois held that public education was mandatory until the age of sixteen; after that, a kid could do whatever he wanted until he was eighteen, at which time he was required to register for military service. It was the high school dropouts who got drafted right away; but for two years these guys got to sleep late and spend their afternoons and evenings hanging out at the bowling alley, betting on games, and gorging themselves on Italian beef sandwiches. At night they would go to Uptown Bowl, where the big, often televised professional matches took place.

The announcer for these events was usually Whispering Ray Rayburn, a small, weaselish man who wore a terrible brown toupee and pencil-line mustache. His ability to speak into a microphone at a consistently low but adequately audible decibel level was his claim to fame. Kids, including myself, often imitated Whispering Ray as they toed the mark preparatory to and as they took their three- or four-step approach before releasing the bowling ball:

"Zabrofsky casually talcs his right hand," a kid would whisper to himself as he stood at the ball rack, "slips three digits into the custom-fit Brunswick Black Beauty, hefts the sixteen-pound spheroid"—(one of Whispering Ray's favorite words for the ball was "spheroid")—"balances it delicately in the palm of his left hand. Amazing how Zabrofsky handles the ebony orb"—("orb" was another pet name)—"almost daintily, as if it were an egg. Now Zabrofsky steps to his spot, feet tight together. He needs this spare to keep pace with the leader, Lars Grotwitz. Zabrofsky studies the five-ten split that confronts him with the kind of concentration Einstein must have mustered to unmuzzle an atom." ("Muster" was also big in Whispering Ray's lexicon.) "Zabrofsky's breathing is all we can hear now. Remember, fans, Big Earl is an asthmatic who depends heavily on the use of an inhaler in order to compete. You can see the impression it makes in the left rear pocket of his Dacron slacks. Despite this serious handicap his intensity is impressive. He begins his approach: one, two, three, the ball swings back and as Big Earl slides forward on the fourth step the powerful form smoothly sets his spheroid on its way. Zabrofsky's velvet touch has set the ebony orb hurtling toward the kingpin. At the last instant it veers left as if by remote control, brushes the five as it whizzes past and hips it toward the ten. Ticked almost too softly, the ten wobbles like an habitué dismounting a stool at Johnny Fazio's Tavern"—(Johnny Fazio was a sponsor of the local TV broadcasts)—"then tumbles into the gutter! Zabrofsky makes the tough spare."

On the last Saturday in February, the league awarded trophies to be presented personally to each team member by Carmen Salvino, a national champion bowler. My team had won its division despite my low pin total. Each team had on its roster at least one novice bowler, leaving it up to the more experienced members to "carry" him, which my team had managed to do. I was grateful to my older teammates for their guidance, patience, and encouragement, and thanks to them I was to be awarded a trophy. The only guy on the team who had not been particularly generous toward me was Oscar Fomento, who worked part-time as a pinsetter. Fomento, not to my displeasure, had left the team two weeks into the league season, after having beaten up his parents with a bowling pin when they gave him a hard time about ditching school. One of the other guys told me Oscar had been sent to a reformatory in Colorado where they shaved his head and made him milk cows in below-freezing temperatures. "That's tough," my teammate said, "but just think how strong Fomento's fingers'll be when he gets back."

My dad had not made it to any of the Saturday morning matches, so I called him on Friday night before the last day of the league and told him this would be his final chance to see me bowl, and that Carmen Salvino would be there giving out trophies. I didn't tell Dad that I'd be receiving a trophy because I wanted him to be surprised. "Salvino," my Dad said. "Yeah, I know the guy. Okay, son."

It snowed heavily late Friday night and into Saturday morning. I had to be at Nortown Bowl by nine and flurries were still coming down at five-to when I kicked my way on a shortcut through fresh white drifts in the alley between Rockwell and Maplewood. Dashing up the steep wet steps I worried about Carmen Salvino and my father being able to drive there. I lived a block away, so it was easy for me and most of the other kids to walk over. I hoped the snowplows were out early clearing the roads.

During the games I kept watching for my dad. Toward the end of the last line there was a lot of shouting: Carmen Salvino had arrived. Our team finished up and went over with the other kids to the counter area, behind which hundreds of pairs of used bowling shoes, sizes two to twenty, were kept in cubbyholes similar to mail slots at hotel desks. Carmen Salvino, a tall, hairy-armed man with thick eyebrows and a head of hair the color and consistency of a major oil slick, stood behind the counter in front of the smelly, worn, multicolored bowling shoes between the Durkee brothers, Dominic and Don, owners of Nortown Bowl.

Dominic and Don Durkee were both about five foot six and had hair only on the sides of their heads, sparse blue threads around the ears. They were grinning like madmen because the great Carmen Salvino was standing next to them in their establishment. The Durkees' skulls shone bright pink under the rude fluorescent lights. The reflection from the top of Carmen Salvino's head blinded anyone foolish enough to stare at it for more than a couple of seconds.

I was the last kid to be presented a trophy. When Carmen Salvino gave it to me he shook my small, naked hand with his huge, hairy one. I noticed, however, that he had extremely long, slender fingers, like a concert pianist's. "Congrajalayshuns, son," he said to me. Then Carmen Salvino turned to Dominic Durkee and asked, "So, we done now?"

When I walked back home through the alley from Maplewood to Rockwell, the snow was still perfectly white and piled high in front of the garages. At home I put my trophy on the top of my dresser. It was the first one I had ever received. The trophy wasn't very big but I really liked the golden figure of a man holding a golden bowling ball, his right arm cocked back. He didn't look at all like Carmen Salvino, or like me, either. He resembled my next-door neighbor Jimmy McLaughlin, an older kid who worked as a dishwasher at Kow Kow's Chinese restaurant on the corner of Devon and Rockwell. Jimmy worked all day Saturday, I knew. I decided I'd take the trophy over later and show it to him.

The Aerodynamics of an Irishman

There was a man who lived on my block when I was a kid whose name was Rooney Sullavan. He would often come walking down the street while the kids were playing ball in front of my house or Johnny McLaughlin's house. Rooney would always stop and ask if he'd ever shown us how he used to throw the knuckleball back when he pitched for Kankakee in 1930.

"Plenty of times, Rooney," Billy Cunningham would say. "No knuckles about it, right?" Tommy Ryan would say. "No knuckles about it, right!" Rooney Sullavan would say. "Give it here and I'll show you." One of us would reluctantly toss Rooney the ball and we'd step up so he could demonstrate for the fortieth time how he held the ball by his fingertips only, no knuckles about it.

"Don't know how it ever got the name knuckler," Rooney'd say. "I call mine the Rooneyball." Then he'd tell one of us, usually Billy because he had the catcher's glove—the old fat-heeled kind that didn't bend unless somebody stepped on it, a big black mitt that Billy's dad had handed down to him from his days at Kankakee or Rock Island or someplace—to get sixty feet away so Rooney could see if he could still "make it wrinkle."

Billy would pace off twelve squares of sidewalk, each

square being approximately five feet long, the length of one nine year old boy's body stretched head to toe lying flat, squat down, and stick his big black glove out in front of his face. With his right hand he'd cover his crotch in case the pitch got away and short-hopped off the cement where he couldn't block it with the mitt. The knuckleball was unpredictable, not even Rooney could tell what would happen once he let it go.

"It's the air makes it hop," Rooney claimed. His leather jacket creaked as he bent, wound up, rotated his right arm like nobody'd done since Chief Bender, crossed his runny gray eyes, and released the ball from the tips of his fingers. We watched as it sailed straight up at first, then sort of floated on an invisible wave before plunging the last ten feet like a balloon that had been pierced by a dart.

Billy always went down on his knees, the back of his right hand stiffened over his crotch, and stuck out his gloved hand at the slowly whirling Rooneyball. Just before it got to Billy's mitt the ball would give out entirely and sink rapidly, inducing Billy to lean forward in order to catch it, only he couldn't because at the last instant it would take a final, sneaky hop before bouncing surprisingly hard off of Billy's unprotected chest.

"*Just* like I told you," Rooney Sullavan would exclaim. "All it takes is plain old air."

Billy would come up with the ball in his upturned glove, his right hand rubbing the place on his chest where the pitch had hit. "You all right, son?" Rooney would ask, and Billy would nod. "Tough kid," Rooney'd say. "I'd like to stay out with you fellas all day, but I got responsibilities." Rooney would muss up Billy's hair with the hand that held the secret to the Rooneyball and walk away whistling "When Irish Eyes Are Smiling" or "My Wild Irish Rose." Rooney was about forty-five or fifty years old and lived with his mother in a bungalow at the corner. He worked nights for Wanzer Dairy, washing out returned milk bottles.

Tommy Ryan would grab the ball out of Billy's mitt and hold it by the tips of his fingers like Rooney Sullavan did, and Billy would go sit on the stoop in front of the closest house and rub his chest. "No way," Tommy would say, considering the prospect of his ever duplicating Rooney's feat. "There must be something he's not telling us."

A Rainy Day at the Nortown Theater

When I was about nine or ten years old my dad picked me up from school one day and took me to the movies. I didn't see him very often since my parents were divorced and I lived with my mother. This day my dad asked me what I wanted to do and since it was raining hard we decided to go see *Dragnet* starring Jack Webb and an Alan Ladd picture, *Shane*.

I had already seen *Dragnet* twice and since it wasn't such a great movie I was really interested in seeing *Shane*, which I'd already seen as well, but only once, and had liked it, especially the end where the kid, Brandon de Wilde, goes running through the bulrushes calling for Shane to come back, "Come back, Shane! Shane, come back!" I had really remembered that scene and was anxious to see it again, so all during *Dragnet* I kept still because I thought my dad wanted to see it, not having already seen it, and when *Shane* came on I was happy.

But it was Wednesday and my dad had promised my mother he'd have me home for dinner at six, so at about a quarter to, like I had dreaded in the back of my head, my dad said we had to go.

"But Dad," I said "*Shane's* not over till six-thirty and I want to see the end where the kid goes running after him yelling, 'Come back, Shane!' That's the best part!"

But my dad said no, we had to go, so I got up and went with him but walked slowly backward up the aisle to see as much of the picture as I could even though I knew now I wasn't going to get to see the end, and we were in the lobby, which was dark and red with gold curtains, and saw it was still pouring outside. My dad made me put on my coat and duck my head down into it when we made a run for the car, which was parked not very far away.

My dad drove me home and talked to me but I didn't hear what he said. I was thinking about the kid who would be running after Shane in about ten more minutes. I kissed my dad good-bye and went in to eat dinner but I stood in the hall and watched him drive off before I did.

Renoir's Chemin montant dans les hautes herbes

The path on the hillside is a stripe of light, a three-dimensional effect. There is nothing theoretical about this: everything is where it is supposed to be. Not merely light and shadow and balance and color but the unprepared for, the element that informs as well as verifies the work. As the light in the Salle Caillebotte in the Jeu de Paume changes the painting changes, too—like the sun slowly emerging from behind a cloud, it opens and displays more of itself.

The people and the setting are from a previous century: women and children descending the path. There is absolutely nothing savage about the picture. Flowers, fruit trees, foot-worn path, wooden fence—nothing to disturb. The element of feeling is calm; difficulty disappears.

An early summer afternoon in the house in Chicago. I'm ten years old. The sky is very dark. A thunderstorm. I'm sitting on the floor in my room, the cool tiles. The rain comes, at first very hard, then soft. I'm playing a game by myself. Nobody else is around, except, perhaps, my mother, in another part of the house. There is and will be for a while nothing to disturb me. This is my most beloved childhood memory, an absolutely inviolable moment, totally devoid of difficulty. It's the same feeling I have when I look at Renoir's *Chemin montant dans les hautes herbes*. I doubt very seriously if my father would have understood this feeling.

Wyoming

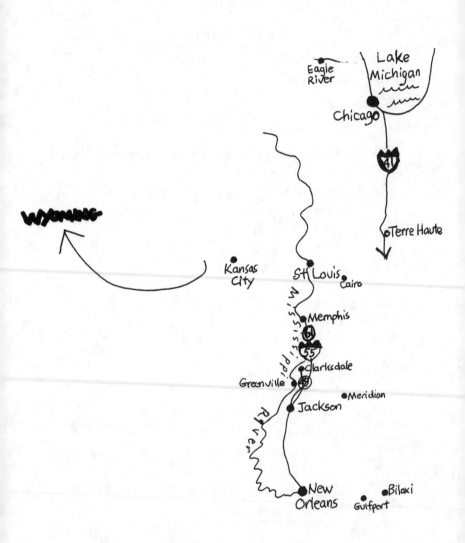

Cobratown

"We're really fine when we're together, aren't we? I mean, when it's just the two of us."

"Uh-huh. How long till we get to the reptile farm?"

"Oh, less than an hour, I think."

"Will they have a giant king cobra, like on the sign?"

"I'm sure they will, sweetheart."

"I hope it's not asleep when we get there. Mom, do cobras sleep?"

"Of course, snakes have to sleep just like people. At least I think they do."

"Do they think?"

"Who, baby?"

"Snakes. Do they have a brain?"

"Yes. They think about food, mostly. What they're going to eat next in order to survive."

"They only think about eating?"

"That's the main thing. And finding a warm, safe place to sleep."

"Some snakes live in trees, on the branches. That can't be so safe. Birds can get them."

"They wait on the limbs for prey, some smaller creature to come along and the snake can snatch it up, or drop on it and wrap itself around and squeeze it to death or until it passes out from not having enough air to breathe. Then the snake crushes it and devours it."

"You're a good driver, aren't you, Mom? You like to drive."

"I'm a very good driver, Roy. I like to drive when we go on long trips together."

"How far is it from Key West to Mississippi?"

"Well, to Jackson, where we're going, it's a pretty long way. Several hundred miles. We go north through Florida, then across Alabama to Mississippi and up to Jackson, which is about in the middle of the state."

"Will Dad be there?"

"No, honey. Your dad is in Chicago. At least I think he is. He could be away somewhere on business."

"Who are we going to see in Mississippi?"

"A good friend of Mommy's. A man named Bert."

"Why is Bert in Mississippi?"

"That's where he lives, baby. He owns a hotel in Jackson."

"What's the name of the hotel?"

"The Prince Rupert."

"Is it like the Casa Azul?"

"I think Bert's hotel is bigger."

"You've never seen it?"

"No, only a photo of it on a postcard that Bert sent."

"How old is Bert?"

"I'm not sure. I guess about forty."

"How old is Dad?"

"Forty-three. He'll be forty-four next month, on the tenth of April."

"Will he invite me to his birthday party?"

"I don't know if your dad will have a birthday party, Roy, but I'm sure he would invite you if he did."

"Some dinosaurs had two brains, Mom, do you know that?"

"Two brains?"

"Yeah, there's a picture in my dinosaur book that Dad sent me that shows how the really big ones had a regular-size brain in their head and a small one in their tail. The really big ones. It's because it was so far from their head to their tail there was too much for only one brain to think about, so God gave them two."

"Who told you God gave dinosaurs two brains?"

"Nanny."

"Your grandmother doesn't know anything about dinosaurs."

"What about Bert?"

"What about him?"

"Do you think he knows about dinosaurs?"

"You'll have to ask him, baby. I don't really know what Bert knows about."

"You said he was your friend."

"Yes, he is."

"Why don't I know him?"

"He's kind of a new friend. That's why I'm taking you to Jackson, to meet Bert, so he can be your friend, too."

"Is Bert a friend of Dad's?"

"No, baby. Dad doesn't know Bert."

"How far now to the reptile farm?"

"We're pretty close. The last sign said twenty-six miles. I can't go too fast on this road."

"I like this car, Mom. I like that it's blue and white, like the sky, except now there's dark clouds."

"It's called a Holiday."

"We're on a holiday now, right?"

"Yes, Roy, it's a kind of holiday. Just taking a little trip, the two of us."

"We're pals, huh?"

"We sure are, baby. You're my best pal."

"Better than Bert?"

"Yes, darling, better than anyone else. You'll always be my favorite boy."

"Look, Mom! We must be really close now."

"The sign said, 'Ten minutes to Cobratown.'"

"If it rains hard, will the snakes stay inside?"

"It's only raining a little, Roy. They'll be out. They'll all be out, baby, don't worry. There'll be cobras crawling all over Cobratown, just for us. You'll see."

Chinese Down the Amazon

"What do you think, baby? Does this place look all right to you?"

"Is it safe?"

"Safe as any motel room in Alabama can be, I guess. At least it looks clean."

"And it doesn't stink of old cigarettes, like the last one."

"We can stay here."

"I'm tired, Mom."

"Take off your shoes and lie down, baby. I'll go out and bring back something for dinner. I'll bet there's a Chinese restaurant in this town. There's Chinese everywhere, Roy, you know that? Even down the Amazon it said in the *National Geographic*. I can get some egg rolls and pork chow mein and egg foo yung. What do you think, baby? Would you like some chow mein and egg foo yung? I'll just make a quick stop in the bathroom first. Out in a jiffy."

"Could I get a Coca-Cola?"

"Oh! Oh, Christ! This is disgusting! Come on, baby, we're moving."

"What happened, Mom?"

"Just filth! The bathroom is crazy with cockroaches! Even the toilet's filled with bugs!"

"I don't see any bugs on the bed."

"Those kind come out later, when the light's off. Get off of there! The beds are probably infested, too. Let's go!"

"I've got to put on my shoes."

"You can do it in the car. Come on!"

"Mom?"

"Yes, Roy?"

"Could I get a hamburger instead of Chinese?"

Bandages

"I was very shy when I was a girl, so shy it was painful. When I had to leave my room at school, to go to class, I often became physically ill. I got sick at the thought of having to see people, or their having to see me, to talk to them. I think this is why I had my skin problems, my eczema. It came from nerves. Being sick allowed me to stay by myself, wrapped up in bandages. People left me alone."

"But weren't you lonely?"

"Not really. I liked to read and listen to the radio and dream. I didn't have to be asleep to really dream, to go into another world where I wasn't afraid of meeting people, of having them look at me and judge me. I really felt better, safe, inside those bandages. They were my shield, I suppose, my protection."

"Prince Valiant has a shield."

"I like this song, Roy. Listen, I'll turn it up: Dean Martin singing 'Ain't Love a Kick in the Head.' He works hard to sound so casual, so relaxed. I always had the feeling Dean Martin was really very shy, like me. That he affected this style of not seeming to care, to be so cool, in order to cover up his real feelings. That's his shield."

"Are we still in Indiana?"

"Yes, baby. We'll be in Indianapolis soon. We'll stay there tonight."

"Indiana goes on a long time."

"It seems that way sometimes. Look out the window. Maybe you'll see a farmer."

"Mom, are there still Indians in Indiana?"

"I don't think so, baby. They all moved away."

"Then why is it still called Indiana, if there aren't any Indians left?"

"Just because they were here before. There were Indians, many different tribes, all over the country."

"The Indians rode horses. They didn't have cars."

"Some of them had cars after."

"After what?"

"After people came from Europe."

"They brought cars from Europe?"

"Yes, but they made them here, too. That's where the Indians got them, the same as everybody else."

"There aren't so many horses here as in Florida."

"Probably not."

"Mom?"

"Yes, Roy?"

"You still wrap yourself up with bandages sometimes."

"When I have an attack of eczema, to cover the ointment I put on the sores, so I don't get everything greasy."

"You don't want anyone to see the sores?"

"One time, not long after I married your father, I had such a bad attack that my skin turned red and black, and I had to stay in the hospital for a month. The sores got so bad they bled. The skin on my arms and hands and face stank under the bandages. I couldn't wash and I smelled terrible. When the nurses unwrapped the bandages to sponge me off, the odor made me want to vomit.

"One day your dad's brother, Uncle Bruno, was there when the nurses took off the bandages. He didn't believe I was really sick, I don't know why, but he wanted to see for himself. It was costing your dad a lot of money for doctors to take care of me and to keep me in a private hospital. When they removed my bandages, Bruno was horrified by the sight of my skin. He couldn't stand the smell or to look at me, and he ran out of the room. I guess he was worried about all the money your father was spending on me. He probably thought I was pretending to be so sick. After that, he said to your dad, 'Kitty used to be so beautiful. What happened to her?'"

"But you are beautiful, Mom."

"I wasn't then, baby, not when I was so sick. I looked pretty bad. But Bruno knew I wasn't faking. I screamed when the nurse peeled off the bandages, my skin stuck to them. Bruno heard me. He wanted your dad to get rid of me, I was too much trouble."

"Did Dad want to get rid of you?"

"No, baby, he didn't. We separated for other reasons."

"Was I a reason?"

"No, sweetheart, of course you weren't. Your father loves you more than anything, just like I do. You mustn't ever think that. The trouble was just between your dad and me, it had nothing to do with you. Really, you're the most precious thing to both of us."

"When will we get to Chicago?"

"Tomorrow afternoon."

"Where are we going to stay? At Nanny's house?"

"No, baby, we'll stay at the hotel, the same place as before.

Remember how you like the chocolate sundaes they make in the restaurant there?"

"Uh-huh. Can we sit in the big booth by the window when we have breakfast?"

"Sure, baby."

"Can I have a chocolate sundae for breakfast?"

"One time you can, okay?"

"Okay."

"Mom?"

"Huh?"

"Do I have nerves?"

"What do you mean, baby? Everyone has nerves."

"I mean, will I ever have to be wrapped up in bandages because of my nerves?"

"No, Roy, you won't. You're not nervous like I was, like I sometimes get now only not so bad as when I was younger. It'll never happen to you, never. Don't worry."

"I love you, Mom. I hope you never have sores and have to get wrapped up again."

"I hope so, too, baby. And remember, I love you more than anything."

Soul Talk

"Mom, when birds die, what happens to their souls?"

"What made you think of that, Roy?"

"I was watching a couple of crows fly by."

"You think birds have souls?"

"That's what Nanny says."

"What do you think the soul is, baby?"

"Something inside a person."

"Where inside?"

"Around the middle."

"You mean by the heart?"

"I don't know. Someplace deep. Can a doctor see it on an X-ray?"

"No, baby, nobody can see it. Sometimes you can feel your soul yourself. It's just a feeling. Not everybody has one."

"Some people don't have a soul?"

"I don't know, Roy, but there are more than a few I'll bet have never been in touch with theirs. Or who'd recognize it if it glowed in the dark."

"Can you see your soul in the dark if you take off all your clothes and look in the mirror?"

"Only if your eyes are closed."

"Mom, that doesn't make sense."

"I hate to tell you this, baby, but the older you get and the more you figure things should make sense, they more than sometimes don't."

"Your soul flies away like a crow when you die and hides in a cloud. When it rains that means the clouds are full of souls and some of 'em are squeezed out. Rain is the dead souls there's no more room for in heaven."

"Did Nanny tell you this, Roy?"

"No, it's just something I thought."

"Baby, there's no way I'll ever think about rain the same way again."

Skylark

"You know, sometimes you look just like your father, only much more beautiful, of course."

"You don't think Dad is beautiful?"

"No, your father isn't so beautiful, but he's a real man."

"And I'm a real boy, like Pinocchio wanted to be."

"Yes, baby, you're a real boy."

"Why isn't Dad with us so much anymore?"

"He's very busy, Roy, you know that. His business takes up most of his time."

"When will I see him again?"

"We'll go to Havana in two weeks and meet him there. You like the hotel where his apartment is, remember? The Nacional?"

"Will the little man with the curly white dog be there?"

"Little man? Oh, Mr. Lipsky. I don't know, baby. Remember the last time we saw him? In Miami, the day after the big hurricane."

"We were walking down the middle of the street that looked like it was covered with diamonds, and Mr. Lipsky was carrying his dog."

"The hurricane had blown out most of the windows of the big hotels, and Collins Avenue was paved with chunks of glass."

"Mr. Lipsky kissed you. I remember he had to stand on his toes. Then he gave me a piece of candy."

"He was carrying his tiny dog because he didn't want him to cut his paws on the broken glass. Mr. Lipsky said the dog was used to taking a walk every morning at that time and he didn't want to disappoint him."

"Mr. Lipsky talks funny."

"What do you mean, he talks funny?"

"He sings."

"Sings?"

"Like he's singing a little song when he says something to you."

"Sure, baby, I know what you mean. Mr. Lipsky's a little odd, but he's been a good friend to your dad and us."

"Does Mr. Lipsky have a wife?"

"I think so, but I've never met her."

"I hope when I grow up I won't be as little as him."

"As *he*, honey. As little as *he*. Of course you won't. You'll be as tall as your dad, or taller."

"Is Mr. Lipsky rich?"

"Why do you ask that, baby?"

"Because he always wears those big sparkly rings."

"Well, Roy, Mr. Lipsky is probably one of the wealthiest men in America."

"How did he get so rich?"

"Oh, he has lots of different kinds of businesses, here and in Cuba. All over the world, maybe."

"What kinds of businesses?"

"Lots of times he gives people money to start a business, and then they have to pay him back more than the amount he gave them or pay him part of what they earn for as long as the business lasts."

"I guess he's pretty smart."

"Your dad thinks Mr. Lipsky is the smartest man he's ever met."

"I hope I'm smart."

"You are, Roy. Don't worry about being smart."

"You know what, Mom?"

"What, baby?"

"I think if I had to choose one thing, to be tall or to be smart, I'd take smart."

"You'll be both, sweetheart, you won't have to choose."

"Do you know what Mr. Lipsky's dog's name is?"

"Sky something, isn't it? Skylark, that's it, like the Hoagy Carmichael song."

"I bet he's smart, too. A dog named Skylark would have to be very smart."

Flamingos

"Mom, after I die I want to come back as a flamingo."

"You won't die for a very long time, Roy. It's too soon to be thinking about it. But I'm not so sure that after people die they come back at all. How do you know about reincarnation? And why a flamingo?"

"How do I know about what?"

"Reincarnation. Like you said, some people believe that after they die they'll return in a different form, as another person or even as an insect or animal."

"Mammy Yerma told me it could happen."

"Mammy Yerma usually knows what she's talking about, but I'm not so sure about being reincarnated, even as a flamingo."

"Flamingos are the most beautiful birds, like the ones around the pond at the racetrack in Hialeah. I'd like to be a dark pink flamingo with a really long, curvy neck."

"They're elegant birds, baby, that's for sure."

"If you could come back as an animal, Mom, what would you be?"

"A leopard, probably. Certainly a big cat of some kind, if I had a choice. Leopards are strong and fast and beautiful. They climb trees, Roy, did you know that? Leopards are terrifically agile."

"What's agile?"

"They're great leapers, with perfect balance. They can jump up in a tree and walk along a narrow limb better than the best acrobat. Another thing about leopards, I believe, is that they mate for life."

"What's that mean?"

"It means once a male and female leopard start a family, they stay together until they die."

"People do, too."

"Yes, baby, some people do. But I think it's harder for human beings to remain true to one another than it is for leopards."

"Why?"

"Well, all animals have to worry about is getting food, protecting their young, and to avoid being eaten by bigger animals. Humans have much more to deal with, plus our brain is different. A leopard acts more on instinct, what he feels. A person uses his brain to reason, to decide what to do."

"I'd like to be a leopard with a human brain. Then I could leap up in a tree and read a book and nobody would bother me because they'd be afraid."

"Baby, are you getting hungry? We humans have to decide if we want to stop soon and eat."

"A leopard would probably eat a flamingo, if he was hungry enough."

"Maybe, but a skinny bird doesn't make much of a meal, and I don't think a leopard would want to mess with all of those feathers."

"Mom, I need to go to the bathroom."

"Now that's something neither a leopard nor a flamingo would think twice about. I'll stop at the next exit. I need to go, too."

Wyoming

"What's your favorite place, Mom?"

"Oh, I have a lot of favorite places, Roy. Cuba, Jamaica, Mexico."

"Is there a place that's really perfect? Somewhere you'd go if you had to spend the rest of your life there and didn't want anyone to find you?"

"How do you know that, baby?"

"Know what?"

"That sometimes I think about going someplace where nobody can find me."

"Even me?"

"No, honey, not you. We'd be together, wherever it might be."

"How about Wyoming?"

"Wyoming?"

"Have you ever been there?"

"Your dad and I were in Sun Valley once, but that's in Idaho. No, Roy, I don't think so. Why?"

"It's really big there, with lots of room to run. I looked on a map. Wyoming's probably a good place to have a dog."

"I'm sure it is, baby. You'd like to have a dog, huh?"

"It wouldn't have to be a big dog, Mom. Even a medium-size or small dog would be okay."

"When I was a little girl we had a chow named Toy, a big

black Chinese dog with a long purple tongue. Toy loved everyone in the family, especially me, and he would have defended us to the death. He was dangerous to anyone outside the house, and not only to people.

"One day Nanny found two dead cats hanging over the back fence in our yard. She didn't know where they came from, and she buried them. The next day or the day after that, she found two or three more dead cats hanging over the fence. It turned out that Toy was killing the neighborhood cats and draping them over the fence to show us. After that, he had to wear a muzzle."

"What's a muzzle?"

"A mask over his mouth, so he couldn't bite. He was a great dog, though, to me. Toy loved the snow when we lived in Illinois. He loved to roll in it and sleep outside on the front porch in the winter. His long fur coat kept him warm."

"What happened to Toy?"

"He ran after a milk truck one day and was hit by a car and killed. This happened just after I went away to school. The deliveryman said that Toy was trying to bite him through the muzzle."

"Does it snow in Wyoming?"

"Oh, yes, baby, it snows a lot in Wyoming. It gets very cold there."

"Toy would have liked it."

"I'm sure he would."

"Mom, can we drive to Wyoming?"

"You mean now?"

"Uh-huh. Is it far?"

"Very far. We're almost to Georgia."

"Can we go someday?"

"Sure, Roy, we'll go."

"We won't tell anyone, right, Mom?"

"No, baby, nobody will know where we are."

"And we'll have a dog."

"I don't see why not."

"From now on when anything bad happens, I'm going to think about Wyoming. Running with my dog."

"It's a good thing, baby. Everybody needs Wyoming."

Saving the Planet

"Mom, what would happen if there was no sun?"

"People couldn't live, plants wouldn't grow. The planet would freeze and become a gigantic ball of ice."

"In school they said the earth is shaped like a pear, not round like a ball."

"So it would be a huge frozen pear spinning out of control. The planets in our solar system revolve around the sun, Roy. If the sun burned out, Earth and Mars and Venus and Saturn and all the others would just be hurtling through space until they crashed into meteors or one another."

"Will it ever happen?"

"What, baby?"

"That there won't be any sun?"

"I don't think so. Not in our lifetime, anyway. Oh, Roy, look at the horses! Nothing is more beautiful than horses running in open country like that."

"Dad's never going to live with us again, is he?"

"I'm not sure, baby. We'll have to wait and see. You'll see your father, though, no matter what."

"I know, Mom. I just hope you're right about the sun not burning out."

A Nice Day on the Ocean

"You know that friend of Dad's with one eye that's always mostly closed?"

"Buzzy Shy. His real name is Enzo Buozzi. What about him?"

"A waiter at the Saxony said Buzzy wanted to give him five dollars to let him kiss his fly."

"Who told you that?"

"I heard him tell Eddie C."

"Heard who?"

"Freddy, the waiter. Why would Buzzy want to kiss Freddy's fly?"

"Did Buzzy ever touch you, Roy?"

"He pinched me once on the cheek when I brought him a cigar Dad gave me to hand him. He gave me a quarter, then tried to pinch my face again, but I got away. It hurt."

"Buzzy Shy is sick, baby. Stay away from him. Promise?"

"Promise. He doesn't look sick."

"The sickness is in his brain, so you can't see it."

"Eddie C. said for *ten* dollars Buzzy could kiss his ass and anything else."

"Who's Eddie C.?"

"A lifeguard. I think at the Spearfish."

"These aren't nice boys, Roy. I don't want you talking to them."

"I wasn't talking to them, Mom, I was listening."

"Don't listen to them, either. I'll talk to your dad about it. I don't want Buzzy Shy bothering you."

"Dad and Buzzy are friends."

"Not really. Buzzy helps out sometimes, that's all."

"How did his eye get like that?"

"He was a prizefighter. Somebody shut it for him."

"Maybe his brain got hurt, too."

"I don't know, baby. He was probably born with the problem in his head. Don't go near him again."

"Mom?"

"Yes, baby?"

"I like the sky like this, when it's really red with only a tiny yellow line under it."

"Red sky at night, sailor's delight. Red sky at morning, sailor take warning."

"What's that mean?"

"Tomorrow will be a nice day on the ocean."

"Sailor's Delight would be a good name for a red Popsicle, don't you think, Mom?"

"Yes, Roy, I do. Remember to tell your dad. I'm sure he knows someone in the Popsicle business."

Perfect Spanish

"Before you were born, I got very sick and your dad made me go to Cuba to recover. I stayed in a lovely house on a beach next to a lavish estate. It was a perfect cure for me, lying in the sun, without responsibilities."

"Was Dad with you?"

"No, I was alone. There was a Chinese couple who took care of the house and me. Chang and Li were their names."

"How long were you there?"

"Six weeks. I was so happy, just by myself, reading, resting, swimming in the Caribbean Sea. It really was the best time of my life. I never felt better, until, of course, I had to leave."

"Why did you have to leave?"

"To make sure you were a healthy baby. I needed to be near my doctor, who was in Chicago."

"The ground is so beautiful here, Mom. It looks like snow, but the air is very hot."

"That's cotton, baby. Cotton is the main crop in Alabama. The temperature doesn't stay high long enough up north to grow it there. Also, the cost of labor is much cheaper in the South, and picking cotton is extremely labor-intensive."

"What does that mean?"

"It takes a lot of people to handpick the buds. That's why slaves were brought here from Africa, to work in the fields."

"They didn't want to come."

"No, baby, they didn't."

"There aren't slaves now, though, right?"

"Not officially, no. But too many people still live almost the same way as they did a hundred or more years ago. There's no work here, really, except in the cottonfields, and it doesn't pay much. The difference between then and now is that people are free to come and go, they're not owned by another person."

"I wouldn't like to be owned by someone."

"Nobody does. Slavery is against the law in the United States, but it still exists in some parts of the world."

"Let's not go there."

"We won't, Roy, I promise."

"Were there slaves in Cuba?"

"At one time, yes."

"Were there slaves when you were there before I was born?"

"No, baby, that was only a few years ago."

"Chang and Li weren't slaves, right?"

"Certainly not. They were caretakers of the property. Chang and Li were very happy to be working there. They were wonderful people and very kind to me."

"How did they get from China to Cuba?"

"I don't know. By boat, probably. Or maybe their parents came from China and Chang and Li were born in Cuba. They spoke perfect Spanish.

"Roy?"

"Yeah, Mom?"

"Are you all right?"

"I'm okay."

"Something's bothering you, I can tell. What is it?"

"I think I'd like to learn to speak perfect Spanish."

"You can, baby. You can start taking Spanish lessons whenever you want."

"Mom?"

"Yes, sweetheart?"

"I bet the slaves didn't think the cotton fields were so beautiful."

Seconds

"Are we going to see Pops and Nanny soon?"

"Yes, baby, we'll be in New Orleans for three or four days, then we'll go to Miami. I don't know if Pops will be there, but Nanny will."

"Why isn't Pops there so much?"

"I never told you this before, but I think you're old enough now to understand. Pops and Nanny haven't always been together. There was a time when I was a girl—more than ten years, in fact—when they were each married to another person."

"Who were they married to?"

"Nanny's husband was a man named Tim O'Malley. His family was in the trucking business in Chicago. Pops married a woman named Sally Price, and they lived in Kansas City. I used to go down on the train and visit them there. This was from when I was the age you are now until I went away to college."

"Why did they marry other people?"

"In those days Pops was a traveling salesman for a shoe company, and Kansas City was part of his territory. Sally was a girlfriend of his for a couple of years before Pops and Nanny got divorced. When he decided to spend more time with Sally than with Nanny, my mother divorced him and she married O'Malley, who'd always liked her."

"So O'Malley was like your other father."

"In a way, but we were never close. I lived most of the time at boarding school, Our Lady of Angelic Desire, so I didn't really see him so much. He died suddenly of a heart attack ten years to the day after he and your grandmother were married."

"How did she and Pops get back together?"

"Pops had divorced Sally two years before O'Malley's death and moved back to Illinois. He always loved my mother and would stand across the street sometimes to watch her come out of our house and get in her car and drive away. Pops wanted Nanny back, and after O'Malley was gone, she agreed to remarry him."

"I bet you were happy."

"No, I wasn't particularly happy, because I didn't completely understand why Pops had left in the first place. O'Malley was nothing special to me, and he wasn't as smart or funny or handsome as my father, but my mother blamed Pops for their separation and I guess I took her side, right or wrong. I don't feel the same way now. It's difficult to know what really goes on between people in a marriage, and I don't think anyone other than those two people can understand, including their children."

"What about you and Dad?"

"What about us, Roy?"

"You're divorced but you're still friends, aren't you?"

"Oh, yes, baby, your dad and I are very good friends. We're better friends now than when we were married."

"And you both love me."

"Of course, baby. Both your dad and I would do anything for you."

"It's okay with me that you and Dad don't live together, but sometimes I get afraid that I won't see him anymore."

"You can see your dad whenever you like. When we get to the hotel in New Orleans, we'll call him, okay? I think he's in Las Vegas now. Maybe he can come to see us before he goes back to Chicago."

"Yeah, Mom, let's call him. Remember the last time we were with him in New Orleans and he ate too many oysters and got so sick?"

"We'll make sure he doesn't eat oysters this time, don't worry. Try to sleep a little now, baby. I'll wake you up when we get there."

Roy's World

"Remember the time you caught a barracuda and brought it back to the hotel and asked Pete the chef to cook it for you?"

"It was the first fish I ever caught. I was out with Uncle Jack on Captain Jimmy's boat, fishing for grouper, but a 'cuda took my mullet."

"Pete thought you were so cute, bringing the barracuda wrapped in newspaper into the kitchen. You were only five then."

"He told me that barracudas aren't good eating, so he made me a kingfish instead."

"Grilled in butter and garlic."

"And he said he wouldn't charge us for it since I'd brought him a fish to trade."

"You really love your Uncle Jack, don't you, baby?"

"He's a great fisherman, and he knows everything about boats."

"You know he was a commander in the navy?"

"Sure, he told me about how he built bridges and navy bases in the Pacific during the war."

"Uncle Jack is a civil and mechanical engineer, Roy. He can draw plans, too, like an architect. He was a Seabee, and the navy offered to make him an admiral if he stayed in."

"Why didn't he?"

"He said to make money it was better to be in private industry. That's why he moved to Florida, to build houses. My brother can do anything, though."

"He can't fly."

"What do you mean, baby? You mean like Superman?"

"No, Uncle Jack told me he tried to become a pilot in the navy. They sent him to Texas to learn how to fly, but he washed out. He said there was something wrong with his ears that made him lose his balance."

"Yes, that's right. I remember when he came home from Texas. He was so disappointed. But Jack can do so many things. You know, baby, if you get really interested in something, you should follow it through all the way. I mean, find out everything you can, learn all there is to learn about it, try to do it or figure it out. That's what your Uncle Jack does, that's how come he knows so much about different things. He can't do everything so well, like flying a plane, but he tries. And you know he's been practically all over the world. Jack's a great traveler."

"I'm going to be a great traveler, too. We travel a lot, don't we, Mom?"

"Yes, we do, but except for Cuba and Mexico, only in the United States."

"I like to draw maps."

"You mean to copy them from the atlas?"

"Sometimes, just to learn where places are. But also I like to make countries up. Oceans and seas, too. It's fun to invent a world nobody else knows."

"What's your favorite country that you made up?"

"Turbania. It's full of tribes of warriors who're always

fighting to take over all of Turbania. The largest tribe is the Forestani. They live in the mountains and come down to attack the Vashtis and Saladites, who are desert people."

"Where exactly is Turbania?"

"Between Nafili and Durocq, on the Sea of Kazmir. A really fierce small tribe, the Bazini, live in the port city of Purset. They're very rich because they own the port and have a big wall all around with fortifications not even the Forestanis can penetrate. The Bazinis also have rifles, which the other tribes don't. The Vashtis and Saladites ride horses, black and white Arabians. The Forestanis travel on foot because the woods in the hills are so thick that horses can't get through. And each tribe has its own language, though the Bazinis speak Spanish and maybe English, too, because of the shipping trade. The Forestanis can also speak like birds, which is the way they communicate when they don't want anyone outside the tribe to know what they're saying. It's a secret language that they're forbidden by tribal law to teach outsiders. If a Forestani is caught telling the secret bird language to a person from another tribe, his tongue is cut out and his eardrums are punctured."

"Well, Roy, we'll be in Chattanooga soon. Let's have a snack and you can tell me about some of your other countries. I hope they're not all as terrible as Turbania."

"Turbania's not so terrible, Mom. Wait until you hear about Cortesia, where all the people are blind and they have to walk around with long sticks to protect themselves from bumping into things and each other, so everyone pokes everyone else with their sticks all the time."

Nomads

"Where are we now, Mom?"

"Just outside Centralia, Illinois."

"This is sure a long train."

"I'll turn off the motor. Tell me if you get too cold, Roy, and I'll turn the heater back on."

"It's cold out, but not real cold yet, even though it's almost December. Why is that?"

"Weather is pretty unpredictable sometimes, baby, especially in the spring or fall. But you can bet before too long this part of the country'll be blanketed white."

"How come we never take a train?"

"You took a train a couple of times, don't you remember? When you went up and back to Eagle River, Wisconsin."

"It was fun sleeping overnight on the train, though I didn't really sleep very much. I stayed up looking out the window into the shadows, imagining what might be out there. I like the dark, Mom, especially if I'm protected from it, like through a train window."

"What did you think you could see, Roy?"

"Monsters, of course. Lots of large creatures crunching through the forest. Then I could see campfires, real quick little flashes of smoky light burning up through the trees. I thought maybe it was Indians, the last ones left living in the woods, moving every day and setting up a new camp at night."

"Nomads."

"What's that?"

"Nomads are people who travel all the time—they don't live in one place."

"Is Nomads the name of a tribe?"

"It used to be. They're in the Bible, I think. Now it's just a word used to describe anyone who's constantly changing their place of residence."

"We move around a lot."

"Yes, we do, but we mostly stay in the same places."

"That's what the Plains Indians did. I read that they would come back to the same campgrounds depending on the seasons."

"I think the Indians understood the weather better than most people do now."

"What do you mean, Mom?"

"People live mostly in cities, so they defy the weather. They stay in their buildings and complain when it rains or snows, or that it's too hot or cold. The Indians adjusted better to changes of climate. When it was too warm on the plains, they moved to the mountains, where it was cooler. When it snowed in the mountains, they moved down."

"This train is about the longest I've ever seen."

"Cotton Belt Route. Southern Serves the South. Don't you love to read what's written on the boxcars?"

"Yeah, but what do the letters mean? Like B&O?"

"Baltimore and Ohio. L&N is Louisville and Norfolk, I think. Or maybe it's Louisiana and Norfolk."

"It's almost ending, Mom. I can see the caboose. Start the car."

"It's nice to have heat, huh, Roy? If we were Indians in the old days we would've had to wait on our horses until the train passed."

"We'd be wrapped in blankets, so we wouldn't be too cold."

"I once saw a painting of an Indian riding in a blizzard, his long-braided black hair and blanket covered with ice. Even the pony's mane was frozen."

"I like cars, Mom, but horses are more beautiful. I'd feel more like a real Nomad if I were on a horse instead of in a car. Wouldn't you?"

"I guess so, baby. But it would take us a lot longer to get anywhere."

"Sometimes I don't care how long it takes. And when we get there I'm always a little disappointed."

"Why disappointed?"

"I don't know. Maybe because sometimes it's better to imagine how something or someplace is rather than to have it or be there. That way you won't ever be disappointed when you find out it's not so great as you hoped."

"You're growing up, Roy, you really are. Some people never figure that out."

"Probably the real Nomads knew, and that's why they were always moving."

"It's impossible to avoid being disappointed sometimes, baby, unless you learn to not expect too much."

"I like traveling, Mom. I like it more than being in one place, so maybe I'm learning."

Ducks on the Pond

"Roy! Roll up your window. It's freezing outside."

"I want to leave it open just a little, okay, Mom? I like the feeling when the heater's on high and we can still feel the cold air."

"Amazing how cold it can get in Mississippi, huh, Roy? And it's not even Christmas yet."

"Where are we now?"

"We just passed the Batesville turnoff. We'll stay tonight in Memphis, maybe at the Peabody if we can get a room. Remember that hotel, baby? The one with the ducks on the pond in the lobby."

"There was a kid there the last time who told me he drowned a duck once. Not one of the Peabody ducks."

"Drowned a duck? I didn't know ducks could drown."

"I guess they can. They have to come up for air, like people, only probably not as often."

"I wish I could pass this darn truck. Sorry, Roy, I don't mean to swear, but the driver won't let me get around him. Tell me more about the ducks. Who was it who drowned one?"

"A boy I met at the Peabody Hotel the last time we stayed there. He was older than me, twelve or thirteen, I think."

"It was in March. Bert came up."

"Is Bert still alive?"

"Of course, baby. Why would you ask that?"

"Just wondering. You said he was having trouble with his brain, so I thought maybe it exploded or something."

"He had something growing in his head, that's right. You remembered. I think the doctors took it out."

"Before his brain could explode."

"His brain wouldn't have exploded, baby. At least I don't think so. If the thing that was growing in there got big enough, though, it might have squeezed the inside of Bert's head so much that he wouldn't have been able to think properly. I'll call him when we get to Memphis."

"What if the doctors couldn't get it out?"

"I'm sure they did, Roy, otherwise I would have heard something. I think I can pass now, hold on."

"Mom, where did the seed in Bert's brain come from?"

"Just a sec, baby, let me get back over into the other lane. Okay, what did you say? How did a seed get where?"

"In Bert's brain. The thing that was growing began as a seed, right? How did it get planted there?"

"That's a good question, Roy. I don't think anybody knows exactly, not even the doctors."

"Remember the Johnny Appleseed song? 'Oh, the Lord is good to me, and so I thank the Lord, for giving me the things I need, the sun and the rain and the apple seed. The Lord is good to me.'"

"I like to hear you sing, baby. You have a sweet voice."

"It couldn't have been an apple seed in Bert's head."

"No, it wasn't. Don't think about it anymore, honey. Pretty soon you'll see the ducks on the pond at the Peabody."

"Maybe that kid will be there again."

"I guess it's possible."
"I wouldn't ever try to drown a duck, even if I could."
"No, Roy, I don't believe you ever would."

Sound of the River

"Is it okay if I turn up the radio?"

"Sure, Roy, but not *too* loud. What's playing?"

"I don't know, but I like it."

"Is that a man or a woman who's screaming?"

"He's not screaming, Mom, he's singing. Sometimes he shouts, but it's part of the song. But that's not the part I care about so much. What I really like is the kind of thumping sound behind him, the way it jumps up around his voice sometimes and almost swallows or drowns it or something."

"You mean the rhythm section. It's the part of the band that keeps the beat. They keep the song moving."

"I don't think I've ever heard music like this before. It reminds me of the noise water makes hitting against the rocks on the side of the river, like down behind the Jax brewery. The same sound over and over, only it's not exactly the same."

"That's the Mississippi, baby. Can you remember how the waves sound on the beach in Cuba? The way they slap down on the sand, then make kind of a hushing noise as the water rushes up before rolling back. It's different than the sound of the river in New Orleans."

"I remember being out on a little boat with Uncle Jack and on one side of the boat the water was green and on the other side it was blue. Uncle Jack told me to put my right hand into the water on the starboard side, into the blue, which was really cold. Then he told me to put my left hand into the water on the port side, and it was very warm. He said the cold blue side was the ocean, and the warm green side was the Gulf Stream. Wasn't that near Varadero?"

"No, honey, that was off Key West."

"Where are we now, Mom?"

"Macon, Georgia."

"What's here?"

"Oh, most likely the same as everyplace else. Men and women who don't understand each other and aren't really willing or able to try. Just what this man is shouting about on the radio."

"I think he's saying, 'Lucille, won't you do your sister's will? Oh, Lucille, won't you do your sister's will? Well, you ran away and left, I love you still.'"

"Sounds about right to me."

Red Highway

"You hit one that time, Mom. I felt the bump."

"I can't avoid them all, baby. They crawl out on the road and lie there because the asphalt absorbs heat and they like the warmth. I have to admit I'm not very fond of snakes, but I'm not trying to run them over."

"I know you wouldn't do it on purpose. There are a lot of good ones, like king snakes, who help farmers by eating rodents that destroy crops."

"You've always loved reptiles, Roy. Maybe when you grow up you'll be a herpetologist."

"Is that the big word for reptile handler?"

"Herpetology is the study of snakes, and a herpetologist is a person who studies them."

"There's another one! It must be six feet long. You just missed him."

"They're easier to see when they're crawling, otherwise they blend into the highway here."

"Why is this road dark red? I've never seen a red highway before."

"It must be the earth here, baby, the color of the dirt or clay."

"If it rained now, I wonder if the snakes would all crawl away."

"Probably they'd want to get down into their holes,"

"Why were you so mean to that man in the restaurant back in Montgomery?"

"He said something I didn't care for."

"Did he say it to you?"

"No, Roy, he said it to everyone who could hear him. He *wanted* people to hear him."

"What was it that he said?"

"He was showing off his ignorance."

"Nobody likes a show-off."

"Especially not his kind."

"What was he showing off about?"

"He used some words I don't like."

"He called you beautiful. 'What's the matter, beautiful?' he said."

"That wasn't what upset me. It was what he said before. Forget about him, honey. God punishes those people."

"Could God change him into a snake and make him crawl out on the red highway so he'd get run over?"

"Roy, don't believe you're better than anybody else because of the way you look or who your parents are, or for any other reason you had nothing to do with directly. Okay?"

"Okay."

"It sounds simple, but it's not so easy to do. Treat people the way you'd like them to treat you, and if you don't have anything good to say, don't say anything."

"Uh-huh."

"Sorry, baby, I don't mean to preach, but that man made me angry."

"Watch out, Mom, there's another snake!"

Lucky

"It's always raining in Indiana."

"Seems that way, doesn't it, baby?"

"I remember one night we were driving through Indiana like this and I saw a sign that said New Monster. Lucky was with us, and I asked him what it meant, and he told me there was a new monster loose around there and the sign was put up to warn people. I imagined a crazyman had escaped from an asylum, or a dangerous freak had run away from the sideshow of a carnival. I was really frightened and stayed awake for a long time staring out the window watching for the monster, even though it was dark."

"Poor Lucky. He was the one who wound up in an asylum."

"You told me he had to go to a hospital."

"He did, Roy, a special kind of hospital for people who can't control themselves."

"Lucky couldn't control himself?"

"In some ways, baby. He told terrible lies to people in business and got into trouble all the time. You know how handsome Lucky was, and he could play the piano so well and sing. When he was a young man he'd been a great athlete, too. He was a wonderful golfer and tennis player and swimmer. Lucky charmed everyone, men and women loved him, but he was insane."

"Later, Lucky told me the name on the sign was really New *Munster*, which is a town in Indiana. He was just joking around with me, Mom. That wasn't such a bad thing, even though I got so scared."

"No, of course not, baby. Lucky stole a lot of money from a big company he was working for, but he didn't go to jail for that, they let him off easy. Then a few weeks later he was arrested for taking off all of his clothes in front of some young girls in a park. I guess he'd done things like that before, or he tried to do something with one of the girls, I can't remember, so this time he was committed to an institution."

"Do you know where Lucky is now?"

"I think he's still locked up in Dunning."

"Where's Dunning?"

"A place outside Chicago."

"How long does he have to stay there?"

"Oh, Roy, who knows? I suppose until he's well. It's really terrible about Lucky, it wasn't his fault. He just couldn't control himself."

"Lucky liked to eat spaghetti with a spoon. He'd chop up his noodles with a knife and then eat them with a tablespoon. Do you remember that, Mom? I think that's a crazy way to eat spaghetti."

K.C. So Far
(Seconds/alternate take)

"How come we've never been to Kansas City before?"

"I used to come here often when I was a girl. From when I was your age until I was seventeen. I rode the train back and forth from Chicago to see my father."

"Pops was in Kansas City then?"

"Yes, for a few years, when he was married to another woman. Remember, I told you about her. Actually, I don't think they were really married. They lived together and she told people they were married. I never liked her."

"What was her name?"

"I called her Aunt Sally. She was a terrible housekeeper, very sloppy. She left her clothes lying around everywhere, always had dirty dishes piled in the sink. My father liked her because she was pretty and well-read. Sally liked to talk about politics, literature, art. She wasn't stupid, I'll say that for her. She was a chain-smoker. The ashtrays in that house were always overflowing with butts and dead matches."

"It's hot here."

"It can get very hot in Kansas City, Roy, especially in the summer. We used to sit out on the porch at three and four o'clock in the morning, drinking lemonade with shaved ice, when we couldn't sleep because of the heat."

"What did Pops do in Kansas City?"

"He was a hat salesman. He traveled all over the Midwest. Traveling salesmen were still called 'drummers' back then. It's where the phrase 'drumming up business' comes from. Or maybe the word 'drummer' came from the saying, I'm not sure. I think Pops had a girlfriend in every town in his territory, or most of them. That's what caused the breakup with Aunt Sally."

"Pops still wears a hat when he's outside."

"Yes, baby, a homburg, that's his favorite. Pops always was a sharp dresser."

"What happened to her?"

"Who? Sally?"

"Yeah."

"You know, I have no idea where she is now, and I doubt that Pops does, either. She stayed in Kansas City for a while after my father moved back to Chicago, then he stopped talking about her. Sally was a blonde with plenty of pep. I bet she found herself a guy and cut Pops off cold. It's strange how sometimes people can be such a large part of your life and then suddenly they're gone. I didn't miss her or those long, hot train trips."

"She wasn't nice to you, huh?"

"Sally wasn't bad to me. I guess I didn't want to like her because I was so close to Nanny, and I felt if I allowed myself to really like Sally then I would be disloyal to my mother. I'm sure most kids have the same conflict."

"If Dad got a new wife, would you want me to hate her?"

"Not at all, baby, of course not. You'd make up your own mind about her. It would depend on how she treated you."

"Even if she was nice and I loved her, I wouldn't love her the same as I love you, Mom. I'm sure I wouldn't."

"Roy, look at that airplane landing! It's coming in so low. The Kansas City airport is in the middle of the city. Planes fly in right over the houses."

"I'd be scared one would crash on us if we lived in a house here. You know, Mom, I don't think I like Kansas City so far."

Concertina Locomotion

"Sometimes it seems like things go very fast, and sometimes they go slower than an inchworm."

"Yes, honey, strange the way time moves, isn't it? I can't believe I'm not twenty or twenty-one or -two anymore. Years get lost, they fly by and you can't remember them. This is when you get older, of course. I'm sure that now you can remember almost exactly when everything happened."

"I like watching snakes crawl, the way their bodies fold and bend and curl up like a lasso, then straighten out."

"Time works sort of like that, in concertina locomotion."

"Is that a train?"

"No, Roy, it's the way some creatures move, especially tree snakes. They kind of coil and partially uncoil and this motion propels them. I read about it in a nature magazine. You know how a concertina or accordion takes in and lets out air when it's being played? Well, this type of snake looks like that."

"Snakes can see where they're going, can't they?"

"Sure, and they use their tongues as sensors."

"The car's headlights are kind of our sensors."

"I also read that blind people use hand gestures when they talk, the same as people who can see. Isn't that interesting? It has something to do with the way human beings think."

"I think Texas goes on forever."

"We just take it a little bit at a time."

"Like concertina locomotion."

"Yes, baby. As soon as we're east of Houston we'll get a whiff of the bayou. You'll know when we're there with your eyes closed."

Imagine

"Roy, do you remember the name of that man in Havana who used to give you a silver dollar whenever he saw you?"

"Sure, Winky. He had two tattoos of a naked girl on his arm."

"Winky Nervo, that's right. It was driving me nuts not being able to remember his name. Winky was in a dream I had last night. What do you mean, he had two tattoos of a naked girl? The same girl?"

"I think so. On one side of the muscle part of his right arm he had the front of the girl and on the underneath was the back of her. She had her hands on her hips the same way in both of the tattoos. I liked Winky a lot. He used to give silver dollars to all the kids."

"For some reason, Winky was in my dream. He was talking to a black woman outside of a restaurant or a bar or a night-club somewhere, maybe in Havana, though it could have been Mexico City. There was a red and yellow sign flashing on and off behind them. The woman's dress was bright blue, and Winky stood very close to her. Under her, almost. You know how little Winky was, and the woman was very black and much taller. She leaned over him like a coconut palm.

"I liked Winky, too. Your dad said he was a terrible gambler, threw everything he had away on craps and the horses."

"Why don't we ever see Winky anymore, Mom?"

"Oh, baby, Winky's someplace nobody can find him. He owed a pile of dough to some wrong guys and couldn't pay it back."

"Maybe he's in the old country. Winky always said how when he got set he would go back to the old country and not do anything but eat and drink and forget."

"Honey, Winky's in a country even older than the one he was talking about."

"Maybe he was showing the woman his tattoos. Winky could make the girl's titties jump when he made a muscle."

"Remind me to call your dad tonight when we get to Tampa. You haven't spoken to him for a while."

"Not since my birthday. Mom?"

"Yes, Roy?"

"Winky always had lots of silver dollars in his pockets."

"That doesn't mean he had money, baby. Not real money, anyway."

"Does Dad have real money?"

"He might not have it, but he knows how to find it and where to get it, and that's almost as good. There's a big difference between your father and a man like Winky Nervo. Don't worry about your dad."

"I won't."

"Winky wasn't sharp, Roy. He didn't think ahead."

"It's important, huh? To think ahead."

"Baby, you can't imagine."

The Geography of Heaven

"Do you realize, Roy, that Cairo, Illinois, where we are now, is actually closer to the state of Mississippi than it is to Chicago?"

"I know we're next to the Mississippi River."

"That's right. We were on the Mississippi in St. Louis, Missouri, and now Cairo. From here it flows down to Memphis. What state is Memphis in, baby?"

"Tennessee."

"Good. Then it goes to Greenville—"

"Mississippi."

"Then to New Orleans—"

"Louisiana."

"Before flowing into—"

"The Gulf of Mexico."

"Great, Roy! You really know your geography."

"I think this is the best way to learn it, Mom, by traveling all over. The places are real, then, instead of just dots and names on a map."

"You should show me your maps, Roy, the ones you made up. I'd like to see them."

"I draw maps of real places too, Mom, not just imaginary ones. When we stop, I'll make a map of all the places we've been. Where are we going to stay tonight?"

"I thought we'd see if we could get to A Little Bit O'

Heaven, in Kentucky. Remember, they have all those little cottages named after different flowers?"

"Oh, yeah. We stayed in the Rose Cottage because that's Nanny's name."

"There certainly isn't much color in the sky today, is there? It's just grey with tiny specks of black in it."

"It might snow, huh?"

"I think it's more likely to rain, honey. It's not cold enough to snow."

"Mom, if you had a choice between freezing to death or burning up, which one would you choose?"

"I'd take freezing, definitely, because once your body is numb all over, you can't feel anything. You die, sure, but it's better than feeling your flesh melt off the bones. How about you?"

"I like being in hot weather a lot more than cold weather, but I guess you're right. I saw in a movie where a guy who was lost in the wilderness made a blanket of snow for himself and survived until the rescuers came because his body stayed warm under the snow."

"I didn't know about that, Roy. Let's remember it, just in case we get stranded sometime in the mountains in a blizzard."

"You were right, Mom, here comes the rain. All the tiny black spots in the sky were raindrops ready to fall. I never saw rain that looked so black before. It's like being bombed by billions of ants."

"Yes, baby, it is strange, isn't it? Roll up your window all the way. I hope we can make it to A Little Bit O' Heaven before it gets too bad."

"Mom, is there a religion of geography?"

"Not really, unless you consider the ones where people worship places they believe an extraordinary event occurred."

"Probably something important to someone happened just about everywhere, and some people made more of a big deal about it than others."

"Yes, baby, you've got it right."

Man and Fate

"Vicksburg is really a sad place, Mom, I've never seen so many graves."

"It's spooky here, baby, I agree. It breaks my heart to think about all the young boys, many not too much older than you, who're buried here. You know, Roy, some people would think we're crazy, driving around like this in a cemetery in Mississippi in the rain. I can't help but imagine the lives these boys might have had if there hadn't been a War Between the States. A civil war is the worst kind of war. It's been almost one hundred years since this one ended, and the South still hasn't recovered."

"Soldiers from the North are buried here, too, Mom. Hundreds of 'em."

"How can a place be so dreary and beautiful at the same time?"

"I'll bet there are ghosts here who come out and fight the war all over again every night."

"It wouldn't surprise me, baby. Somebody could make a terrific movie of ghosts or even corpses rising from their graves and not fighting but talking with one another peacefully about how horribly wrong it was to have a war in the first place."

"That wouldn't be so exciting, Mom, not if they were just talking. It would be cool to see the corpses, though."

"The only real reasons people go to war anymore are religion and money, and often it's a combination of the two. In the Civil War, cheap labor in the form of slaves was the main issue. In World War II, Hitler used the Jews as scapegoats for Germany's economic problems, which were a result of World War I. He had to go to war to get Germany out of debt. Do you understand any of this, Roy?"

"Not everything. I know that sometimes people want the land that other people are on."

"That has to do with money. One piece of land might be better than another to grow crops on, or there's oil or gas or diamonds and gold or other valuable minerals in it. And as far as religion is concerned, everybody should be left alone and leave others alone to worship as they please."

"Why don't they?"

"Most do, Roy, but some people get carried away. They believe their way should be the only way. It's when people think they've got an exclusive on being right that the world goes ape."

"I once heard Dad say to a guy, 'If I had to get a job done right and I had to choose between you and an ape to do it, I'd take the ape.'"

"I've had enough of Vicksburg, baby. How about you?"

Where Osceola Lives

"Mom, did you know that the Seminoles are the only Indian tribe that never gave up? They hid out here in the Everglades and the soldiers couldn't defeat them."

"I know that the Glades was much larger then, so the Indians had more room to move around and evade the army."

"The Seminoles weren't really a regular tribe, either. They were made up of renegades and survivors of several different tribes who banded together for a last stand in what they called the Terrible Place. Their leader was Osceola, whose real name was Billy Powell, and he was mostly a white man."

"If I'm not mistaken, Roy, the road to Miami that we're on now was originally a Micosukee Indian trail. Imagine how difficult it must have been to build the highway here."

"Really dangerous, too. There's alligators and panthers and water moccasins all around. The Seminoles somehow survived everything, even swamp fevers that killed dozens of soldiers."

"In the movie *Key Largo*, there are two Seminole brothers who've escaped from jail and the cops are looking for them. Even though he's seen them passing in a canoe, the hotel owner doesn't tell the cops because he likes the brothers and believes they were treated unfairly. Later, just before a hurricane is about to hit, the Seminole brothers and other Indians come to the hotel for shelter, as they'd always done during a big storm, but a gangster who's taken over the hotel refuses to let them in."

"What happens to them?"

"They huddle together on the porch of the hotel and ride it out. The Seminole brothers survive."

"Remember Johnny Sugarland, my favorite alligator wrestler at the reptile farm up in St. Augustine?"

"Sure, baby. The boy with three fingers on one hand and the thumb missing on the other."

"He's a Seminole. Johnny told me about Osceola, so I got a book about him from the school library. Nobody except the Seminoles knows where Osceola's body is buried. Some of them say that Osceola is still alive and hunting with an eagle, an owl, and a one-eyed dog as old as he is way back in a part of the Terrible Place that no white man has ever seen."

"Crazy Horse, the Sioux warrior, is another Indian whose burial place is kept secret. Supposedly, no white man knows where his grave is, either."

"I'd go into the swamp with Johnny, if he'd take me. It would be great to see where Osceola lives."

"I'm sure he's dead now, Roy. For the Seminoles, it's Osceola's spirit that's still alive."

"I think I like the Everglades more than any other place I've been."

"Why is that, baby?"

"It's got the most hiding places of anywhere. If you don't get eaten by a gator or a snake, or get swallowed up in quicksand or die of a fever, you could disappear from everyone for as long as you wanted."

"Roy, there's a reason the Indians called this the Terrible Place."

"I know, Mom, but I think I'd be okay, as long as I remembered the way out."

The Crime of Pass Christian

"You know, Mom, the best time for me is when we're moving in the car. I like it when we're between the places we're coming from and going to."

"Don't you miss your friends, or sleeping in your own bed?"

"Sometimes. But right now we're not in New Orleans yet and it's kind of great that nobody else knows exactly where we are. Where are we, anyway?"

"Comin' up on Pass Christian, honey. Remember once we stayed in a house here for a week when your dad had business in Biloxi? An old two-story house with a big screened-in porch that wrapped all around the second floor."

"It's where I trapped a big brown scorpion under a glass and left it there overnight. In the morning the glass was still upside down but the scorpion was gone. You let it go when I was asleep, didn't you, Mom?"

"No, baby, I told you I didn't. I don't know how it got out. And your dad was away that night in New Orleans. It was a real mystery."

"I like that we don't know what happened. Maybe there's a ghost living in the house who picked up the glass, or somehow the scorpion did it with his poison tail."

"This part of the Gulf Coast always seems haunted to me.

If the scorpion had gotten out by itself, the glass would have fallen over, or at least moved. As I recall, it was in exactly the same place the next morning when we looked."

"What kind of ghost do you think lives in that house?"

"Oh, probably the old lady who lived there all of her life. Someone told me she was almost a hundred years old when she died. She never married, and lived alone after her parents passed away."

"What was her name?"

"Baby, I don't remember. Mabel something, I think. There was a story about a kidnapping involving the woman. I can't recall exactly what happened, but she had been kidnapped when she was a child and held for ransom. The family was quite wealthy. It was a famous case."

"Did the police catch the kidnappers?"

"I guess so. Oh, wait, Roy, here's the sharp curve in the highway I hate. I always forget when it's coming up."

"You're a great driver, Mom. I always feel safe in the car with you."

"You shouldn't ever worry when we're driving, baby. Now, look, the road stays pretty straight from here on. Yes, the men who kidnapped Mabel Wildrose—that was the family's name, Wildrose—were caught and sent to prison."

"Did they hurt her?"

"Something bad happened, but it was strange. Mabel Wildrose was nine years old when she was kidnapped."

"The same age as me."

"Yes, your age. They cut off some of little Mabel's hair and sent it to her parents."

"She must have been really scared."

"I'm sure she was. But other than that, I don't think she was harmed. Her parents paid the money and the cops found Mabel wherever it was the kidnappers said she would be."

"You said the men were caught."

"Uh-huh, in New Orleans, when they tried to get on a freighter bound for South America. There was one crazy part of the deal I remember now: The men had left her wrapped in a blanket, and when they were caught trying to board the boat at the dock in New Orleans, one of them was discovered to be carrying Mabel's clothes, including her shoes, in his suitcase. The man had polished the shoes and asked the police if he could keep them with him in his jail cell. He was a nut."

"I wouldn't want to be kidnapped."

"Baby, nobody's going to steal you. Everyone knows who your dad is. They wouldn't want to get into trouble with him."

"What if they didn't want money? What if someone wanted to keep me?"

"It won't happen, Roy, really. Don't worry."

"One day I thought I saw a ghost in the house in Pass Christian, but I don't think it was Mabel Wildrose. It was too big to be her. I was lying on the floor in the front room, playing with my soldiers. It was rainy and kind of dark and cold, and a shadow ran through the room and went out the door. I didn't really see it, it was more like I felt it. The screen door flew open and banged shut behind the shadow."

"Probably only the wind, baby, blowing through the house."

"It might have been the ghost of one of the kidnappers, maybe the guy with Mabel's shoes. Do you think they're dead now?"

"Who, honey?"

"The men who stole Mabel Wildrose when she was nine."

"Oh, they've been dead a long time. They probably died in prison."

"I'd stab someone with my knife if he tried to take me. I'd try to get him in the eye. Probably Mabel didn't have a knife on her, huh, Mom?"

"I doubt that she did, Roy, but sometimes there's not much you can do to stop a person, especially if they're bigger than you."

"I'd wait until they weren't looking and then stab my knife in their eye and run away. They wouldn't catch me if I got outside."

"Forget about it, baby. Nobody is going to kidnap you."

"Sure, Mom, I know. But I'm gonna keep my knife on me anyway."

Cool Breeze

"What would you do if one of the men on the chain gang broke away and jumped in our car?"

"That won't happen, Roy. We won't be stopped much longer. Their leg irons are too tough to bust, and these prisoners are swinging bush hooks, not sledgehammers."

"The air is so smoky here. It must be really hard for the men to breathe when it's so hot."

"We're in the Bessemer Cutoff, baby. This part of Alabama is full of steel mills. If these men weren't prisoners, most of them would be working in the mills or mines or blast furnaces somewhere in Jefferson County."

"There are more black guys than white guys on this chain gang. On the last one we passed, in Georgia, there were more white prisoners."

"We're going to move now, honey. Get your head back in."

"Uncle Jack had two brothers working construction for him who'd been on a chain gang. Their names were Royal and Rayal."

"They told you they were in jail?"

"Uh-huh. They didn't murder anybody, only robbed a bank. Tried to, anyway. Rayal, I think it was, told me the reason they got caught was because they didn't have a car. They got the money, then tried to take a bus to get away."

"Where was this?"

"Jacksonville, I think. The bus didn't arrive when it was supposed to, so the cops arrested them."

"I'll never forget that movie with Paul Muni, *I Was a Fugitive from a Chain Gang*. At the end he escapes, and when he meets his old girlfriend, she asks him how he survives. As he disappears into the shadows, he whispers, 'I steal.' It's pretty spooky."

"I feel kind of bad waving back at the chain-gang guys, you know? We get to leave and they don't."

"Here we go. Oh, baby, doesn't it feel good to have a breeze?"

Night Owl

"It's dangerous to drive in the fog like this, isn't it, Mom?"

"We're going slowly, baby, in case we have to stop on a dime."

"Do you know how many bridges there are that connect the islands between Key West and Miami?"

"About forty, I think, maybe more."

"Does everyone have secrets?"

"Oh, yes, certainly they do."

"Do you?"

"One or two."

"Would you die if anybody found them out?"

"I wouldn't die, no. There are just a few things I'd rather other people didn't know."

"Even me?"

"Even you what?"

"You have secrets you wouldn't tell me?"

"Roy, there are things I don't want to think about or remember, things I try to keep secret even from myself."

"It must be hard to keep a secret from yourself."

"Gee, baby, I can't see a thing."

Islamorada

"Listen, baby, tonight when we get to the hotel I want you to call your dad."

"Is he coming to Miami?"

"No, he has to stay in Chicago. Your dad is sick, Roy, he's in the hospital. It'll cheer him up if you call him there."

"What's wrong with him?"

"He's got a problem with his stomach. I think he needs to have an operation."

"I remember when I was in the hospital to have my tonsils out. You stayed in the room with me on a little bed."

"You were such a good patient. After the surgery you opened your mouth to talk but you couldn't. All you could do was whisper."

"The nurse gave me ice cream."

"Poor baby, when the doctor came in you asked him if he would do another operation and put your voice back in."

"Is Dad scared?"

"Your dad doesn't scare easily, honey. He's a pretty tough guy."

"The doctor said I was brave. I didn't cry or anything."

"You were great, Roy. I was the one who was frightened."

"Can we stop at Mozo's in Islamorada and get squid rings?"

"Sure. Oh, there's a big sailboat, Roy. Look! She's a real beauty."

"It's a ketch."

"I never can tell the difference between a ketch and a yawl."

"The mizzenmast is farther forward on a ketch, and the mizzen sail is larger than on a yawl. Uncle Jack taught me."

"You know, I don't think your dad has ever been on a boat in his life, except when he was a little boy and sailed across the Atlantic Ocean with his family from Europe to America."

"How old was he?"

"About eight, I think."

"Did they come on a sailboat?"

"No, baby, on a big ship with lots of people."

"Why did they come?"

"To have a better life. After the big war, the first one, things were very bad where your dad's family lived."

"Were they poor?"

"I guess it was difficult to make a decent living. There were more opportunities over here. The United States was a young country and people from all over, not just Europe but Asia and Africa, too, felt they could build a new life for themselves. Everyone came to America this way, for work and religious reasons. They still do."

"Were you already here when Dad came?"

"I wasn't born yet. Your dad had been here for almost thirty years before we met."

"Dad didn't tell me he was sick."

"He'll pull through, Roy, don't worry. We'll call him as soon as we get to Miami. You'll see, he'll tell you he's going to be all right."

"I wish you and Dad were still married."

"It's better the way things are for your dad and me, baby. Some people just weren't made to live with each other."

"I won't ever get married."

"Don't be ridiculous, Roy. Of course you'll get married. You'll have children and grandchildren and everything. You just have to find the right girl."

"Weren't you the right girl for Dad?"

"He thought I was. It's not so easy to explain, honey. There were all kinds of reasons our marriage didn't work. The best part of it was that we had you."

"If Dad dies, I don't want another one."

"What do you mean, baby?"

"If you get married again, he won't be my dad."

"Look, Roy. Is that one a ketch or a yawl?"

"A yawl. It's got two jibs."

"We'll be in Islamorada in five minutes. I'm ready for some squid rings myself."

On the Arm

"Maybe we can go to a baseball game in Atlanta. I went once with Dad and his friend Buddy from Detroit. We saw the Crackers play the Pelicans."

"We'll look in the newspaper when we get there, baby, and see if the Crackers are in town. Don't hang out of the window, Roy. Get your arms back in."

"Mom, it's so hot. I won't get hit."

"Remember when we read about that boy whose arm got taken off by a truck?"

"Is Buddy from Detroit still in Atlanta?"

"Buddy Delmar, you mean? No, honey, I think he's in Vegas now. He works for Moe Lipsky."

"Buddy was a ballplayer. He knows a lot about baseball."

"Your dad told me Buddy could have had a career in the game, but he had a problem, so he didn't go on."

"What kind of problem?"

"He's a fixer, Roy. I guess he always was, even back when he played. Buddy bet on games. He paid pitchers to let batters get hits, hitters to strike out, and fielders to make errors."

"Did he get caught?"

"Somewhere along the line. I don't know exactly what happened, but according to your dad, Buddy had an umpire on the arm who had a big mouth. The ump spilled the beans and did Buddy in. I don't think he went to jail over it, but he was finished as far as baseball was concerned."

"He could tell me things that would happen before they happened. A player would do something and Buddy'd say, 'Didn't I tell ya?'"

"The first time I met Buddy Delmar, your dad and I were at the Ambassador, in the Pump Room. Buddy paid for our drinks. He flashed a roll that could have choked a horse."

"You mean if he tried to swallow the money."

"Who, honey?"

"The horse."

"It's just an expression, Roy. Buddy likes to act like a big shot. Some women go for that routine, not me."

"I remember Buddy asked me, 'How's that good-looking mother of yours?'"

"Did your dad hear him say that?"

"I think Dad was getting a hot dog."

"Buddy Delmar thinks he's catnip to the ladies."

"I'd never take money to strike out."

"Of course you wouldn't. You won't be like Buddy Delmar. You'll be your own man."

"Is Dad his own man?"

"Sure, Roy, he is. Being his own man causes him problems sometimes."

"Buddy from Detroit had a problem, you said."

"Baby, you don't have to be like any of these people. Your dad is a decent person, don't get me wrong, but he does things you'll never do. Your life will be different, Roy."

"What about Buddy?"

"What about him?"

"Is he a decent person?"

"If Buddy Delmar had never been born, the world wouldn't be any worse off."

"Mom, if we ever have a house, could I get a dog?"

"Oh, Roy, you really are my own special angel. We won't always be living in hotels, I promise. Listen, if the Crackers aren't playing, we'll go to a movie, okay?"

"Okay. It wouldn't have to be a big dog. If he was too big, he wouldn't be happy riding in our car so much."

"Baby, remember what I said about keeping your arms in."

Look Out Below

"Mom, when you were a girl, what did you want to be when you grew up?"

"I thought I might be a singer, like Nanny. Other than that, I had no idea."

"Uncle Jack says I should be an architect, like him."

"If that's what you want to do, baby."

"I want to be a baseball player, but after that I'm not sure."

"Apalachicola. Doesn't the name of this town sound like a train? Let's say it, Roy. Slowly at first, then faster and faster."

"Apalachicola—Apalachicola—Apalachicola—Apalachicola—Apalachicola—Apalachi-agh!-cola! It gets harder the more times you say it."

"Isn't it just like a choo-choo? *Ap*-alachi-*cola*—*Ap*-alachi-*cola*— *Ap*-alachi-*cola*—"

"It's pretty here, huh, Mom?"

"Especially now, at sundown. Your dad and I were here once in a big storm. Almost a hurricane but not quite. Black sand was flying everywhere. We couldn't see to drive."

"I think it was close to here where Uncle Jack's boat got stuck on a sandbar when he and Skip and I were fishing. Remember, Mom? I told you about it."

"Tell me again, honey. I've forgotten."

"Uncle Jack couldn't drive the boat off the sandbar so he told me and Skip to jump in the water and push from the stern."

"Did it work, or did you have to call the coast guard?"

"It worked, but when we first got in and started pushing, Skip saw a big fin coming at us. He shouted, 'Shark!' and we climbed back into the boat as fast as we could. Uncle Jack asked, 'Where's a shark?' Skip pointed at the place where he'd seen the fin and Uncle Jack said, 'Get back in the water and push! I'll tell you when there's a shark coming.'"

"That sounds like my brother. Did you both get back in?"

"Uh-huh, Skip's a lot stronger than I am—"

"He's four years older."

"Yeah, well, he pushed as hard as he could and so did I, and Uncle Jack cut the wheel sharp so the boat came unstuck. Then Skip and I swam fast to it and climbed aboard before the shark came back."

"I'll have to talk to Jack about this."

"No, Mom, it was okay. We had to do it. We were really stuck and only Uncle Jack could drive the boat."

"You wouldn't be much good as a baseball player if you lost a leg to a shark."

"There was a pitcher with the White Sox who only had one leg. I saw a movie about him. I think he lost it in a war."

"Roy, is this true?"

"Honest, Mom. He pitched on a wooden leg. I don't know how many times, but he did it."

"That's incredible. A person really can do just about anything if he works hard at it."

"When I find out what I want to do, I'll work really hard at it."

"After baseball, you mean."

"Yeah, after baseball. Mom?"

"Yes, baby?"

"Do you think Skip and I were really dumb to get back in the water? What if the shark had come up from underneath to bite us?"

"Please, Roy, even if there was a one-legged baseball player, I don't want to think about it."

The Up and Up

"Why didn't you tell me Dad was going to die?"

"Oh, baby, I didn't know he would die. I mean, everyone dies sooner or later, but we couldn't know he would die this soon."

"Dad wasn't old."

"No, Roy, he was forty-eight. Too young."

"I didn't know he was in the hospital again."

"We talked to him just after he went back in, don't you remember?"

"I forgot."

"Your dad really loved you, Roy, more than anything."

"He didn't sound sick, that's why I didn't remember he was in the hospital."

"It's a shame he died, baby, really a shame."

"After he came home from the hospital the first time, after his operation, Phil Sharky told me Dad was too tough to die."

"Phil Sharky's not a person worth listening to about anything. I'm sure he meant well telling you that, but he's the kind of man who if you ask him to turn off a light only knows how to break the lamp."

"What does that mean, Mom?"

"I mean Phil Sharky can't be trusted. You can't believe a word he says. If he says it's Tuesday, you can get fat betting it's Friday. Phil Sharky's a crooked cop who doesn't play straight with anyone."

"I thought he was Dad's friend."

"Look how dark the sky's getting, Roy, and it's only two o'clock. If we're lucky, we'll make it to Asheville before the rain hits. I thought we'd stay at the Dixieland Hotel. It has the prettiest views of the Smokies."

"Phil Sharky gave me his gun to hold once. It was really heavy. He said to be careful because it was loaded."

"Was your dad there?"

"No, he went out with Dummy Fish and left me at the store. He told me he'd be right back. I asked Phil if the gun wouldn't weigh so much if there weren't any bullets in it and he said if they went where they were supposed to it wouldn't."

"Baby, you won't ever see Phil Sharky again if I have anything to do with it. Did you tell your dad about this? That Phil let you handle his gun?"

"Dad didn't get back for a long time and I fell asleep on the newspaper bundles. When I woke up, Phil was gone and Dad and Dummy and I went to Charmette's for pancakes. I remember because Solly Banks was there and he came over to our table and said I was a lucky kid to have the kind of father who'd take me out for pancakes at four in the morning."

"Suitcase Solly, another character who couldn't tell the up and up if it bit him. So your dad didn't know Sharky showed you the gun?"

"Phil told me not to say anything to Dad, in case he wouldn't like the idea, so I didn't."

"We're not gonna beat the rain, baby, but we'll get there

while there's still light. Tomorrow we'll fly to Chicago. The funeral's on Sunday."

"Will everyone be there?"

"I don't know about everyone, but your dad knew a lot of people. Most of the ones who come will want to talk to you."

"Even people I don't know?"

"Probably. All you have to do is thank them for paying their respects to your father."

"What if I cry?"

"It's normal to cry at a funeral, Roy. Don't worry about it."

"Mom, what was the last thing Dad said before he died?"

"Gee, baby, I really don't know. I think when the nurse came to give him a shot for the pain, he'd already died in his sleep. There was nobody in the room."

"Do you remember the last thing he said to you?"

"Oh, I think it was just to not worry, that he'd be okay."

"I bet Dad knew he was dying and he didn't want to tell us."

"Maybe so."

"What if he got scared just before he died? Nobody was there for him to talk to."

"Don't think about it, Roy. Your dad didn't live very long, but he enjoyed himself."

"Dad was on the up and up, wasn't he, Mom?"

"Your dad did things his own way, but the important thing to remember, baby, is that he knew the difference."

Black Space

"Isn't that terrible? Roy, did you hear that just now on the radio?"

"I wasn't really listening Mom. I'm reading the story of Ferdinand Magellan. Did you know there's a cloud named after him that's a black space in the Milky Way? What happened?"

"They found two cut-up bodies in suitcases in the left-luggage department in the railway station in New Orleans."

"Do they know who put them there?"

"The attendant told police it was a heavyset, middle-aged white woman who wore glasses and a black raincoat with what looked like orange paint stains on it."

"It's raining now. When it rains in Louisiana, everything gets fuzzy."

"What do you mean, things get fuzzy?"

"The drops are wobbly on the windows and that makes shapes outside weird."

"People are capable of anything, baby, you know that? The problem is you can never really know who you're dealing with, like this woman who chopped up those bodies."

"Were they children?"

"Who? The corpses in the suitcases?"

"Uh-huh."

"No, honey, I'm sure they were adults."

"But the crazy lady who did it is loose."

"They'll get her, Roy, don't worry. Maybe not right away, but they will."

"Do you think it's easy to kill someone, Mom?"

"What a strange question to ask. I don't know. I suppose for some people it is."

"Could you do it?"

"Maybe with a gun if I were being threatened. I've never really thought about it."

"Could you cut up a body like she did?"

"Roy, stop it. Of course not. Let's talk about something else. Are you hungry? We can stop in Manchac and get fried catfish at Middendorf's."

"I wonder if she wrapped the body parts up so blood didn't go everywhere."

"Please, baby. I'm sorry I mentioned it."

"Remember the shrunken head Uncle Jack brought back from New Guinea?"

"How could I forget?"

"Somebody had to chop it off before it got shrunk. Or do you think the whole body was shrunk first?"

"Roy, that's enough."

"I bet that attendant was really surprised when he saw what was inside those suitcases."

"They must have begun to smell badly so the attendant got suspicious. I think he called the police, though, and they opened the suitcases."

"Do you think the woman is still in New Orleans?"

"Baby, how would I know? Maybe she just took a train and beat it out of town. I'm sure she did. She's probably in Phoenix, Arizona, by now."

"Nobody really has control over anybody else, do they?"

"A lot of people don't have control over themselves, that's how a horrible thing like this can happen. Now stop thinking about it. Think about horses, Roy, how beautiful they are when they run."

"Mom, you won't leave me alone tonight, okay?"

"No, baby, I won't go out tonight. I promise."

Fear and Desire

"I don't like when the sky gets dark so early."

"That's what happens in the winter, Roy. The days are a lot shorter and colder because our side of the planet is farther away from the sun."

"The trees look beautiful without leaves, don't they, Mom?"

"I like when it's sunny and cold. It makes my skin feel so good. We'll stop soon, baby, in Door County. I'm a little tired."

"I think I dream better in winter."

"Maybe because you sleep more."

"Mom, what do you think of dreams?"

"What do I think of them?"

"Yeah. I mean, what are they? Are they real?"

"Sure, they're real. Sometimes you find out things in dreams that you can't any other way."

"Like what?"

"Some experts think dreams are wishes. You dream about what you really want to happen."

"Once I dreamed that I was running in a forest and wolves were chasing me. There was a real big red wolf that caught me in deep snow and started eating one of my legs. Then I woke up. I didn't want that to happen."

"Maybe it meant something else. Also, dreams depend

on what's happening around you at the time. Dreams are full of symbols."

"What's a symbol?"

"Something that represents something else, like the red wolf in your dream. The red wolf was a symbol of a fear or desire."

"I was afraid of the wolf because I didn't want him to bite me."

"Do you remember anything else about the dream?"

"The red wolf didn't have any eyes, only dark holes where his eyes were supposed to be."

"This sounds like a case for Sigmund Freud."

"Is he a detective?"

"No, baby, he was a doctor who studied dreams and wrote about them."

"If I'd had a gun I would have shot that wolf."

"It's not always so easy to get rid of something that's chasing you, because it's inside your own mind."

"You mean the red wolf is hiding in my brain?"

"Don't worry, Roy, the wolf won't bother you again. You woke up before he could hurt you."

"The sky's all dark now. Mom, is desire bad or good?"

"It can be either, depending on what it is and why a person desires something."

"A person can't decide not to dream."

"No, baby, dreams either come or they don't. We'll stay at the Ojibway Inn. Remember that motel with the Indian chief on the sign?"

"I bet everybody has scary dreams sometimes."

"Of course they do."

"I hope the red wolf is chasing somebody else now."

God's Tornado

"Oh, Roy, I just love this song. I'll turn it up."

"What is it?"

"'Java Jive' by the Ink Spots. Listen: 'I love java sweet and hot, whoops Mr. Moto, I'm a coffee pot.'"

"That's crazy, Mom. What's it mean?"

"'I love the java and the java loves me.' It's just a silly little song that was popular when I was a girl. Coffee's called java because coffee beans come from there."

"Where?"

"The island of Java, near Borneo."

"Borneo's where the wild men are."

"It's part of Indonesia. Coffee wakes you up, makes you feel jivey, you know, jumpy."

"Who's Mr. Moto?"

"Peter Lorre played him in the movies. He was a Japanese detective."

"Why is he in the song?"

"I don't have the faintest, baby. I guess just because he was a popular character at the time, before the war."

"Look, Mom, there's tree branches all over the road."

"Sit back, honey, I don't want you to bump your head."

"There must have been a big windstorm."

"This part of the country is called Tornado Alley. I don't

know why people would live here, especially in trailers. It's always the trailers that get destroyed by tornadoes."

"Where were we when a tornado made all those rocks fall on our car?"

"Kansas. Wasn't that terrible? There were hundreds of dents on the roof and the hood, and we had to get a new windshield."

"Where does weather come from?"

"From everywhere, baby. The wind starts blowing in the middle of the Arabian Sea or the South China Sea or somewhere, and stirs up the waves. Pretty soon there's a storm and clouds form and the planet rotates and spins so the rain or snow works its way around and melts or hardens depending on the temperature."

"Does the temperature depend on how close you are to heaven or hell?"

"No, Roy, heaven and hell have nothing to do with the weather. What matters most is where a place is in relation to the equator."

"I know where that is. It's a line around the globe."

"The nearer to the equator, the hotter it is."

"I think hell must be on the equator, Mom. The ground opens up like a big grave and when the planet turns all the bad people fall in."

"How do good people get to heaven?"

"A whirly wind called God's Tornado comes and picks them up and takes them there. People disappear all the time after a tornado."

"And what about purgatory, the place where people are that God hasn't decided about yet?"

"I think they wait on the planet until God or the Devil chooses them."

"Are they kept in any particular place?"

"I'm not sure. Maybe they just stay where they are, and they don't even know they're waiting."

"I don't know if you know it, baby, but what you say makes perfect sense. I wish I could write down some of these things, or we had a tape recorder to keep them."

"Don't worry, Mom, I've got a good memory. I won't forget anything."

Forever After

MAP OF ROY'S NEIGHBORHOOD

WESTERN AVENUE

ARTESIAN

CAMPBELL

MAPLEWOOD

ROCKWELL

TALMAN

WASHTENAW

FAIRFIELD

CALIFORNIA AVENUE

CANAL

KEDZIE AVENUE

Northtown Theater

Sinclair Station

BIG Roy's House 6135

Nelson's Meat Market

Crawford's Bowling Alley

Roy's House 6312

St. Tim's Church & School

Green Briar Park

Lilac Tree

Clinton School

Caravia (later Funeral Home)

GRANVILLE

FREMONT

GLENLAKE

PETERSON AVENUE

Mather H.S.

DEVON AVENUE

Walgreen's

Robin Hood Restaurant

Roby's Cleaning Station

Pit Restaurant

Rosenfield's

Grandis

Thillens

RED HOT RANCH

Forever After

Riding in a car on a highway late at night was one of Roy's greatest pleasures. In between towns, on dark, sparsely populated roads, Roy enjoyed imagining the lives of these isolated inhabitants, their looks, clothes and habits. He also liked listening to the radio when his mother or father did not feel like talking. Roy and one or the other of his parents spent a considerable amount of time traveling, mostly on the road between Chicago, New Orleans and Miami, the three cities in which they alternately resided.

Roy did not mind this peripatetic existence because it was the only life he knew. When he grew up, Roy thought, he might prefer to remain in one place for more than a couple of months at a time; but for now, being always "on the go," as his mother phrased it, did not displease him. Roy liked meeting new people at the hotels at which they stayed, hearing stories about these strangers' lives in Cincinnati or Houston or Indianapolis. Roy often memorized the names of their dogs and horses, the names of the streets on which they lived, even the numbers on their houses. The only numbers of this nature Roy owned were room numbers at the hotels. When someone asked him where he lived, Roy would respond: "The Roosevelt, room 504," or "The Ambassador, room 309," or "The Delmonico, room 406."

One night when Roy and his father were in southern

Georgia, headed for Ocala, Florida, a report came over the car radio about a manhunt being conducted for a thirty-two year old Negro male named Lavern Rope. Lavern Rope, an unemployed catfish farm worker who until recently had been living in Belzoni, Mississippi, had apparently murdered his mother, then kidnapped a nun, whose car he had stolen. Most of the nun's body was found in the bathtub of a hotel room in Valdosta, not far from where Roy and his father were driving. The nun's left arm was missing, police said, and was assumed to still be in the possession of Lavern Rope, who was last reported seen leaving Vic and Flo's Forever After Drive-in, a popular Valdosta hamburger stand, just past midnight in Sister Mary Alice Gogarty's 1957 red and beige Chrysler Newport convertible.

Roy immediately went on the lookout for the stolen car, though the stretch of highway they were on was pretty lonely at three o'clock in the morning. Only one car had passed them, going the other way, in the last half hour or so, and Roy had not noticed what model it was.

"Dad," said Roy, "why would Lavern Rope keep the nun's left arm?"

"Probably thought it would make the body harder to identify," Roy's father answered. "Maybe she had a tattoo on it."

"I didn't think nuns had tattoos."

"She could have got it before she became a nun."

"He'll probably dump the arm somewhere, Dad, don't you think?"

"I guess. Don't ever get a tattoo, son. There might come a day you won't want to be recognized. It's better if you don't have any identifying marks on your body."

By the time they reached Ocala, the sun was coming up.

Roy's father checked them into a hotel and when they got to their room he asked Roy if he wanted to use the bathroom.

"No, Dad, you can go first."

Roy's father laughed. "What's the matter, son? Afraid there'll be a body in the bathtub?"

"No," said Roy, "just a left arm."

While his father was in the bathroom, Roy thought about Lavern Rope cutting off Sister Mary Alice Gogarty's arm in a Valdosta hotel room. If he had used a pocket knife, it would have taken a very long time. He had probably brought along a kitchen knife from his mother's house to do the job, Roy decided.

When his father came out, Roy asked him, "Do you think the cops will find Lavern Rope?"

"Sure, they'll catch him."

"Dad?"

"Yes, son?"

"I bet they never find the nun's arm."

"Won't make much difference, will it? Come on, boy, take your clothes off. We need to sleep."

Roy undressed and got into one of the two beds. Before Roy could ask another question, his father was snoring in the other bed. Roy lay there with his eyes open for several minutes; then he realized that he needed to go to the bathroom.

Suddenly, his father stopped snoring.

"Son, you still awake?"

"Yes, Dad."

Roy's father sat up in his bed.

"It just occurred to me that a brand new red and beige Chrysler Newport convertible is a damn unusual automobile for a nun to be driving."

The Mason-Dixon Line

One Sunday I accompanied my dad on an automobile trip up from Chicago to Dixon, Illinois. It was a sunny January morning, and it must have been when I was ten years old because I remember that I wore the black leather motorcycle jacket I'd received that Christmas. I was very fond of that jacket with its multitude of bright silver zippers and two silver stars on each epaulet. I also wore a blue cashmere scarf of my dad's and an old pair of brown leather gloves he'd given me after my mother gave him a new pair of calfskins for Christmas.

I liked watching the snowy fields as we sped past them on the narrow, two-lane northern Illinois roads. We passed through a number of little towns, each of them with seemingly identical centers: a Rexall, hardware store, First State Bank of Illinois, Presbyterian, Methodist, and Catholic churches with snowcapped steeples, and a statue of Black Hawk, the heroic Sauk and Fox chief.

When my dad had asked me if I wanted to take a ride with him that morning I'd said sure, without asking where to or why. My dad never asked twice and he never made any promises about when we'd be back. I liked the uncertainty of those situations, the open-endedness about them. Anything could happen, I figured; it was more fun not knowing what to expect.

"We're going to Dixon," Dad said after we'd been driving for about forty-five minutes. "To see a man named Mason." I'd recently read a Young Readers biography of Robert E. Lee, so I knew all about the Civil War. "We're on the Mason-Dixon line," I said, and laughed, pleased with my little kid's idea of a joke. "That's it, boy," said my dad. "We're going to get a line on Mason in Dixon."

The town of Dixon appeared to be one street long, like in a Western movie: the hardware store, bank, church, and drugstore. I didn't see a statue. We went into a tiny café next to the bank that was empty except for a counterman. Dad told me to sit in one of the booths and told the counterman to give me a hot chocolate and whatever else I wanted.

"I'll be back in an hour, son," said Dad. He gave the counterman a twenty-dollar bill and walked out. When the counterman brought over the hot chocolate he asked if there was anything else he could get for me. "A hamburger," I said, "and an order of fries." "You got it," he said.

I sipped slowly at the hot chocolate until he brought me the hamburger and fries. The counterman sat on a stool near the booth and looked at me. "That your old man?" he asked. "He's my dad," I said, between bites of the hamburger. "Any special reason he's here?" he asked. I didn't say anything and the counterman said, "You are from Chi, aren't ya?" I nodded yes and kept chewing. "You must be here for a reason," he said. "My dad needs to see someone," I said. "Thought so," said the counterman. "Know his name?" I took a big bite of the hamburger before I answered. "No," I said. The counterman looked at me, then out the window again. After a minute he walked over behind the counter. "Let me know if ya need anything else," he said.

While my dad was gone I tried to imagine who this fellow Mason was. I figured he must be some guy hiding out from the Chicago cops, and that his real name probably wasn't Mason. My dad came back in less than an hour, picked up his change from the counterman, tipped him, and said to me, "Had enough to eat?" I said yes and followed him out to the car.

"This is an awfully small town," I said to my dad as we drove away. "Does Mason live here?" "Who?" he asked. Then he said, "Oh yeah, Mason." Dad didn't say anything else for a while. He took a cigar out of his overcoat pocket, bit off the tip, rolled down his window, and spit it out before saying, "No he doesn't live here. Just visiting."

We drove along for a few miles before Dad lit his cigar, leaving the window open. I put the scarf up around my face to keep warm and settled back in the seat. My dad drove and didn't talk for about a half hour. Around Marengo he said, "Did that counterman back there ask you any questions?" "He asked me if you were my dad and if we were from Chicago," I said. "What did you tell him?" "I said yes." "Anything else?" "He asked if you were there for any special reason and I said you were there to see someone." "Did you tell him who?" Dad asked. "I said I didn't know his name."

Dad nodded and threw his dead cigar out the window, then rolled it up. "You tired?" he asked. "No," I said. "What do you think," he said, "would you rather live out here or in the city?" "The city," I said. "I think it's more interesting there." "So do I," said Dad. "Relax, son, and we'll be home before you know it."

The Wedding

When my mother married her third husband, I, at the age of eleven, was given the duty, or privilege, of proposing a toast at the banquet following the wedding. My uncle Buck coached me—"Unaccustomed as I am to public speaking," I was to begin.

I kept going over it in my head. "Unaccustomed as I am to public speaking . . ." until the moment arrived and I found myself standing with a glass in my hand saying, "Unaccustomed as I am to public speaking—" I stopped. I couldn't remember what else my uncle had told me to say, so I said, "I want to propose a toast to my new father"—I paused—"and my old mother."

Everybody laughed and applauded. I could hear my uncle's high-pitched twitter. It wasn't what I was supposed to have said, that last part. My mother wasn't old, she was about thirty, and that wasn't what I'd meant by "old." I'd meant she was my same mother, that hadn't changed. No matter how often the father changed the mother did not.

I was afraid I'd insulted her. Everybody laughing was no insurance against that. I didn't want this new father, and a few months later, neither did my mother.

The Pitcher

One night when I was eleven I was playing baseball in the alley behind my house. I was batting left-handed when I hit a tremendous home run that rolled all the way to the end of the alley and would have gone into the street but an old man turning the corner picked it up. The old man came walking up the alley toward me and my friends, flipping the baseball up in the air and catching it. When he got to where we stood, the old man asked us who'd hit that ball.

"I did," I said.

"It was sure a wallop," said the old man, and he stood there, grinning. "I used to play ball," he said, and my friends and I looked at each other. "With the Cardinals, and the Cubs."

My friends and I looked at the ground or down the alley where the cars went by on Rosemont Avenue.

"You don't believe me," said the old man. "Well, look here." And he held out a gold ring in the palm of his hand. "Go on, look at it," he said. I took it. "Read it," said the old man.

"World Series, 1931," I said.

"I was with the Cardinals then," the old guy said, smiling now. "Was a pitcher. These days I'm just an old bird dog, a scout."

I looked up at the old man. "What's your name?" I asked.

"Tony Kaufmann," he said. I gave him his ring back. "You just keep hitting 'em like that, young fella, and you'll be a big leaguer." The old man tossed my friend Billy the ball. "So long," he said, and walked on up to the end of the alley, where he went in the back door of Beebs and Glen's Tavern.

"Think he was tellin' the truth or is he a nut?" one of the kids asked me.

"I don't know," I said, "let's go ask my grandfather. He'd remember him if he really played."

Billy and I ran into my house and found Pops watching TV in his room.

"Do you remember a guy named Tony Kaufmann?" I asked him. "An old guy in the alley just told us he pitched in the World Series."

"He showed us his ring," said Billy.

My grandfather raised his eyebrows. "Tony Kaufmann? In the alley? I remember him. Sure, he used to pitch for the Cubs."

Billy and I looked at each other.

"Where's he now?" asked my grandfather.

"We saw him go into Beebs and Glen's," said Billy.

"Well," said Pops, getting out of his chair, "let's go see what the old-timer has to say."

"You mean you'll take us in the tavern with you?" I asked.

"Come on," said Pops, not even bothering to put on his hat, "never knew a pitcher who could hold his liquor."

A Place in the Sun

The final memory I have of my dad is the time we attended a Chicago Bears football game at Wrigley Field about a month before he died. It was in November of 1958, a cold day, cold even for November on the shore of Lake Michigan. I don't remember what team the Bears were playing that afternoon; mostly I recall the overcast sky, the freezing temperature and visible breath of the players curling out from beneath their helmets like smoke from dragons' nostrils.

My dad was in good spirits despite the fact that the colostomy he'd undergone that previous summer had measurably curtailed his physical activities. He ate heartily at the game, the way he always had: two or three hot dogs, coffee, beer, a few shots of Bushmill's from a flask he kept in an overcoat pocket. He shook hands with a number of men on our way to our seats and again on our way out of the stadium, talking briefly with each of them, laughing and patting them on the back or arm.

Later, however, on our way home, he had to stop the car and get out to vomit on the side of the road. After he'd finished it took him several minutes to compose himself, leaning back against the door until he felt well enough to climb back in behind the wheel. "Don't worry, son," he said to me. "Just a bad stomach, that's all."

During the summer, after my dad got out of the hospital, we'd gone to Florida, where we stayed for a few weeks in a house on Key Biscayne. I had a good time there, swimming in the pool in the yard and watching the boats navigate the narrow canal that ran behind the fence at the rear of the property. I liked waving to and being waved at by the skippers as they guided their sleek white powerboats carefully through the inlet. One afternoon, though, I went into my dad's bedroom to ask him something and I saw him in the bathroom holding the rubber pouch by the hole in his side through which he was forced to evacuate his bowels. He grimaced as he performed the necessary machinations and told me to wait for him outside. He closed the bathroom door and I went back to the pool.

I sat in a beach chair looking out across the inland waterway in the direction of the Atlantic Ocean. I didn't like seeing my dad look so uncomfortable, but I knew there was nothing I could do for him. I tried to remember his stomach the way it was before, before there was a red hole in the side of it, but I couldn't. I could only picture him as he stood in the bathroom moments before with the pain showing in his face.

When he came out he was dressed and smiling. "What do you think, son?" he said. "Should I buy this house? Do you like it here?"

I wanted to ask him how he was feeling now, but I didn't. "Sure, Dad," I said. "It's a great place."

The Winner

My mother and I spent Christmas and New Year's of 1957 in Chicago. By this time, being ten years old and having experienced portions of the northern winter on several occasions, I was prepared for the worst. On our way to Chicago on the long drive from Florida, I excitedly anticipated playing in deep snow and skating on icy ponds. It turned out to be a mild winter, however, very unusual for Chicago in that by Christmas Day there had been no snow.

"The first snowfall is always around Thanksgiving," said Pops, my grandfather. "This year, you didn't need a coat. It's been the longest Indian summer ever."

I didn't mind being able to play outside with the kids who lived on Pops's street, but I couldn't hide my disappointment in not seeing snow, something we certainly did not get in Key West. The neighborhood boys and girls were friendly enough, though I felt like an outsider, even though I'd known some of them from previous visits for as many as three years.

By New Year's Eve it still had not snowed and my mother and I were due to leave on the second of January. I complained to her about this and she said, "Baby, sometimes you just can't win."

I was invited on New Year's Day to the birthday party of a

boy I didn't know very well, Jimmy Kelly, a policeman's son who lived in an apartment in a three-flat at the end of the block. Johnny and Billy Duffy, who lived next door to Pops, persuaded me to come with them. Johnny was my age, Billy one year younger; they were good pals of Kelly's and assured me Kelly and his parents wouldn't mind if I came along. Just to make sure, the Duffy brothers' mother called Jimmy Kelly's mother and she said they'd be happy to have me.

Since the invitation had come at practically the last minute and all of the toy stores were closed because of the holiday, I didn't have a proper present to bring for Jimmy Kelly. My mother put some candy in a bag, wrapped Christmas paper around it, tied on a red ribbon and handed it to me.

"This will be okay," she said. "Just be polite to his parents and thank them for inviting you."

"They didn't invite me," I told her, "Johnny and Billy did. Mrs. Duffy called Kelly's mother."

"Thank them anyway. Have a good time."

At Kelly's house, kids of all ages were running around, screaming and yelling, playing tag, knocking over lamps and tables, driving the family's two black cocker spaniels, Mick and Mack, crazy. The dogs were running with and being trampled by the marauding children. Officer Kelly, in uniform with his gunbelt on, sat in a chair by the front door drinking beer out of a brown bottle. He was a large man, overweight, almost bald. He didn't seem to be at all disturbed by the chaos.

Mrs. Kelly took my gift and the Duffy brothers' gift for Jimmy, said, "Thanks, boys, go on in," and disappeared into the kitchen.

Johnny and Billy and I got going with the others and after a while Mrs. Kelly appeared with a birthday cake and ice cream. The cake had twelve candles on it, eleven for Jimmy's age and one for good luck. Jimmy was a big fat kid and blew all of the candles out in one try with ease. We each ate a piece of chocolate cake with a scoop of vanilla ice cream, then Jimmy opened his gifts. He immediately swallowed most of the candy my mother had put into the bag.

Mrs. Kelly presided over the playing of several games, following each of which she presented the winner with a prize. I won most of these games, and with each successive victory I became increasingly embarrassed. Since I was essentially a stranger, not really a friend of the birthday boy's, the other kids, including Johnny and Billy Duffy, grew somewhat hostile toward me. I felt badly about this, and after winning a third or fourth game decided that was enough—even if I could win another game, I would lose on purpose so as not to further antagonize anyone else.

The next contest, however, was to be the last, and the winner was to receive the grand prize, a brand new professional model football autographed by Bobby Layne, quarterback of the champion Detroit Lions. Officer Kelly, Mrs. Kelly told us, had been given this ball personally by Bobby Layne, whom he had met while providing security for him when the Lions came to Chicago to play the Bears.

The final event was not a game but a raffle. Each child picked a small, folded piece of paper out of Officer Kelly's police hat. A number had been written on every piece of paper by Mrs. Kelly. Officer Kelly had already decided what the winning number would be and himself would announce it following the children's choices.

I took a number and waited, seated on the floor with the other kids, not even bothering to see what number I had chosen. Officer Kelly stood up, holding the football in one huge hand, and looked at the kids, each of whom, except for me, waited eagerly to hear the magic number which they were desperately hoping would be the one they had plucked out of the policeman's hat. Even Jimmy had taken a number.

"Sixteen," said Officer Kelly.

Several of the kids groaned loudly, and they all looked at one another to see who had won the football. None of them had it. Then their heads turned in my direction. There were fifteen other children at the party and all thirty of their eyes burned into mine. Officer and Mrs. Kelly joined them. I imagined Mick and Mack, the cocker spaniels, staring at me, too, their tongues hanging out, waiting to bite me should I admit to holding the precious number sixteen.

I unfolded my piece of paper and there it was: 16. I looked up directly into the empty pale green and yellow eyes of Officer Kelly. I handed him the little piece of paper and he scrutinized it, as if inspecting it for forgery. The kids looked at him, hoping against hope that there had been a mistake, that somehow nobody, especially me, had chosen the winning number.

Officer Kelly raised his eyes from the piece of paper and stared again at me.

"Your father is a Jew, isn't he?" Officer Kelly said.

I didn't answer. Officer Kelly turned to his wife and asked, "Didn't you tell me his old man is a Jew?"

"His mother's a Catholic," said Mrs. Kelly. "Her people are from County Kerry."

"I don't want the football," I said, and stood up. "Jimmy should have it, it's his birthday."

Jimmy got up and grabbed the ball out of his father's hand.

"Let's go play!" he shouted, and ran out the door.

The kids all ran out after him.

I looked at Mrs. Kelly. "Thanks," I said, and started to walk out of the apartment.

"You're forgetting your prizes," said Mrs. Kelly, "the toys you won."

"It's okay," I said.

"Happy New Year!" Mrs. Kelly shouted after me.

When I got home my mother asked if it had been a good party.

"I guess," I said.

She could tell there was something wrong but she didn't push me. That was one good thing about my mother, she knew when to leave me alone. It was getting dark and she went to draw the drapes.

"Oh, baby," she said, "come look out the window. It's snowing."

The God of Birds

While he was waiting to get a haircut at Duke's Barber Shop, Roy was reading an article in a hunting and fishing magazine about a man in Northern Asia who hunted wolves with only a golden eagle as a weapon. This man rode a horse holding on one arm a four-foot long golden eagle around the shore of a mountain lake in a country next to China from November to March looking for prey. Beginning each day before dawn, the eagle master, called a berkutchi, cloaked in a black velvet robe from neck to ankle to protect him from fierce mountain winds, rode out alone with his huge bird. The berkutchi scoffed at those who practiced falconry, said the article in the magazine, deriding it as a sport for children and cowards.

"Eagles are the most magnificent of hunting beasts," said the master. "My eagle has killed many large-horned ibex by shoving them off cliffs. He would fight a man if I commanded him to do so."

The berkutchi's eagle, who was never given a name, had been with him for more than thirty years. He had students, the article said, whom the berkutchi instructed in the ways to capture and train eagles.

"I can only show them how it is done," said the master, "but I would never give away the real secrets. These secrets a man must learn by himself, or he will not become a successful hunter. A man is only a man, but the eagle is the god of birds."

"Roy!" Duke the barber shouted. "Didn't ya hear me? You're next!"

Roy closed the magazine and put it back on the card table in the waiting area.

When he was in the chair, Duke asked him, "Find somethin' interestin' inna magazine, kid?"

"Yes, an article about a guy in the mountains of Asia who hunts wolves on horseback with an eagle."

"How old are you now, Roy?"

"Almost twelve."

"Think you could do that?" Duke asked, as he clipped. "Learn how to hunt with a bird?"

Duke was in his mid-forties, mostly bald, with a three day beard. Roy had never seen Duke clean shaven, even though he was a barber. His shop had three chairs but only one other man worked with him, a Puerto Rican named Alfredito. Alfredito was missing the last three fingers of his right hand, the one in which he held the scissors. When Roy asked him how he'd lost them, Alfredito said a donkey had bitten them off when he was a boy back in Bayamon. Roy never allowed Alfredito to cut his hair anymore because Alfredito always nicked him. He got his hair cut on Thursdays now, which was Alfredito's day off. Duke told Roy that Alfredito worked Thursdays for his brother, Ramon, who had a tailor shop over by Logan Square. Roy wondered if Alfredito could sew better than he could cut hair with only one finger on his right hand.

"I don't know," Roy answered. "Maybe if I grew up there and had a good berkutchi."

"Berkutchi? What's that?"

"An eagle master. The one in the magazine said the eagle is the god of birds."

The door to the shop opened and an old man wearing a gray fedora came in.

"Mr. Majewski, hello," said Duke. "Have a seat, I'll be right with you."

Mr. Majewski stared at Alfredito's empty chair and said, "So where is the Puerto Rican boy?"

"It's Thursday, Mr. Majewski. Alfredito don't work for me on Thursdays."

"He works tomorrow?" asked Mr. Majewski.

"Yeah, he'll be here."

"I'll come tomorrow," Majewski said, and walked out.

"You want it short today, Roy?"

"Leave it long in the back, Duke. I don't like my neck to feel scratchy."

"I used to shoot birds when I was a boy," said Duke, "up in Waukegan."

As he was walking home from the barber shop, a sudden brisk wind caused Roy to put up the collar of his leather jacket. Then it began to rain. Roy walked faster, imagining how terrible the weather could get during the winter months in the mountains of rural Asia. Even a four-foot long golden eagle must sometimes have a difficult time flying against a cold, hard wind hurtling out of the Caucasus, Roy thought, when he saw a gray hat being blown past him down the middle of Blackhawk Avenue. He did not stop to see if it was Mr. Majewski's fedora.

Sundays and Tibor

Roy hated Sundays. Sunday was the day his mother usually chose to pick a fight with her husband or boyfriend of the moment, to express in no unquiet way her dissatisfaction and disappointment with her current situation, making certain that the man in question was left in no doubt as to his responsibility for her distress.

Sunday was also the day his mother insisted on the family, such as it was, going out to dinner. Nothing ever pleased her on these occasions: the route her husband or boyfriend chose to drive to their destination; the service and food at the restaurant; everyone else's bad manners, etc. Roy dreaded these outings. Many times he purposely stayed away from his house, even when he had nobody to play with, there were no games going on at the park, or the weather was particularly foul. He'd walk the streets until he was certain his mother, her husband and his sister had left the house before returning, guaranteeing him two or three hours of solitude. Of course when his mother got home, Roy knew, she would yell at him for missing the family affair, but he had time to prepare an excuse: the game he was playing in went into overtime, or somebody got hurt and Roy had to help him get home.

Holidays were also potential trouble, time bombs set to Roy's mother's internal clock. The bigger the occasion, the louder the ticking. Once, Christmas fell on a Sunday. Christmas also happened to be the anniversary of his mother's marriage to her third husband, the father of Roy's little sister. This triple-barreled day of disaster resulted in his sister's father's belongings being thrown by Roy's mother down the front steps and scattered over the lawn in front of their house. As Roy's soon-no-longer-to-be stepfather picked up his soggy undershorts and other personal items from the snow, Roy, who bore the man no particular affection, felt something close to compassion for him. That day, Roy swore to himself that he would never get married.

For a period of time when his mother was between marriages, when Roy was nine years old, she kept company with a Hungarian named Tibor. Tibor worked as a concierge or receptionist at an elegant little hotel on the near north side of Chicago. He was a short, skinny, hawk-nosed man in his mid-thirties with a mane of unruly brown hair. Where and under what circumstances his mother had made Tibor's acquaintance, Roy never knew. Tibor had fled Budapest at the beginning of the Hungarian revolution. In his home country, apparently, he had been a musician of some kind, although Roy had never heard him play an instrument. Tibor never approached Roy's mother's piano.

One rainy Sunday afternoon in late autumn, Roy returned to his house from playing in a particularly bruising tackle football game. He was looking forward to collapsing on his bed, which was really a fold-out couch, but when he arrived, Tibor was stretched out on it with his shoes and socks off, asleep. Roy's little Admiral portable television set was on. His mother was making something in the kitchen.

"Hey, Ma, Tibor's on my bed."

"He had a long night at the hotel," she said, "it was very busy. He's tired."

"So am I. I wanted to lie down. Why can't Tibor sleep in your room, or on the couch in the living room?"

"He was watching television, Roy. And your room is closer to the kitchen. I'm making him a goulash."

"What's a goulash?"

"A ragout of beef with vegetables cooked with lots of paprika. It's the national dish of Hungary."

"Why don't you wake him up now so he can come in here and eat it?"

"The goulash isn't ready yet. I'll call him when it's done. Tibor had a hard time in Hungary, Roy. He had to escape."

Roy's mother turned and looked at him for the first time since he'd entered the kitchen.

"Your face is filthy," she said. "So are your clothes."

"I was playing football. The field was muddy."

"Roy's mother returned her attention to the goulash. Roy walked out the back door and sat down on the porch stairs.

"Close the door when you go out!" said his mother. "It's cold!"

She closed it.

On another Sunday, Roy was walking behind his mother and Tibor next to Lake Michigan. Tibor was wearing a long, gray overcoat that was too big for him. Roy recognized it as one having belonged to his mother's second husband, Lucious O'Toole, a handsome drunkard she had divorced after six months. Lucious had a metal plate in his head from being wounded in the war and he couldn't hold a job. Years later, when Roy was in high school, he saw Lucious staggering along a downtown street, unshaven, wearing a torn and dirty trenchcoat. It was snowing but Lucious was hatless and, Roy noticed, now mostly bald.

Following his mother and Tibor, Roy thought about pushing Tibor into the lake. Roy didn't hate him, but he wanted Tibor to just disappear and for his mother never to mention Hungary or goulash again.

After Roy saw Lucious O'Toole downtown that day, he told his mother, who showed no emotion.

"He looked like a bum," said Roy.

"You never know what's going to happen to a person," she said. "Sometimes it's better that way."

Poor Children of Israel

"They got Harry the Butcher last night," the Viper told Roy. "Only after he piped a cop, though. I heard it on the radio."

The city had been terrorized for days by a gang of six escapees from the Poor Children of Israel Hospital for the Criminally Insane. Roy had read about them in the headlines of the *Tribune* all week. MADMEN STILL AT LARGE was one. Others were LUNATICS ON CRIME SPREE and TERROR GRIPS CITY AS CRAZY KILLERS ELUDE CAPTURE!

Roy and the Viper trudged through slush on their way to school. After two days of snow, the temperature had risen suddenly, turning the streets into a sloppy mess.

"Where'd they find him?" Roy asked.

"The Butcher and the other five broke into a room at the Edgewater Beach Hotel. A husband and wife were in there. Swede Wolf strangled the guy. The woman ran out to the balcony and tried to climb down from the fourth floor. She was screamin' and yellin' for help. That's how the cops found 'em."

"Did she get away?"

"No, they grabbed her and kept her prisoner for a few hours. The radio didn't say, but I bet those maniacs put it to her. Most of 'em had been locked up for years."

"How'd a bunch like that get upstairs in a big fancy hotel?"

A bus sped through a puddle and splashed muddy water on the boys' coats and pants.

"God damn it!" the Viper shouted. "I'll get that driver with an iceball, you'll see."

"They must have snuck in during the night," said Roy.

"Who was gonna stop 'em? Swede Wolf had murdered all kinds of people. Harry the Butcher, too."

"Did they have guns?"

"No, just crowbars and tire irons. The cops shot the Mahoney twins, the ones who raped and decapitated their mother."

"They cut her head off before they had sex with the body," said Roy. "I remember when it happened."

"Yeah, that's right. Anyway, those two are dead. The rest of 'em were captured. The cop the Butcher laid out is in the hospital. He might not make it."

The other big news Roy heard about that day was that the governor of the state of Georgia had forbidden the Georgia Tech football team to play in the Sugar Bowl on New Year's Day because their opponent, the University of Pittsburgh, had a Negro fullback. Students rioted on the Georgia Tech campus and were hosed down and beaten by Atlanta police.

When Roy got home after school, his mother was sitting at the kitchen table, reading a magazine.

"Hey, Ma, you hear they caught those escaped mental patients at the Edgewater Beach Hotel? They murdered a guy and the cops shot and killed two of them."

"How terrible, Roy," she said, without looking up. "There's some chicken left from last night in the refrigerator, if you're hungry."

Roy looked at the calendar on the wall next to the sink.

The date was December 11, 1955. The calendar was from Nelson's Meat Market on Ojibway Boulevard. The top part was a photograph of the Nelson brothers: Ernie, Dave and Phil. The three of them had white aprons on and they were smiling. Ernie and Phil had mustaches. Dave was the youngest, still in his twenties. His right eye was glass. He'd popped it out and shown it to Roy once and told him Phil had poked his real eye with a toy sword when they were kids.

"What a shame," said Roy's mother. "The Edgewater Beach used to be such a nice hotel."

The Man Who Wanted to
Get the Bad Taste of the World
Out of His Mouth

Roy got thrown out of school on the same day the bodies of the Grimes sisters were found in the Forest Preserve. The Grimes girls were twelve and thirteen, one and two years older than Roy. It was a rainy April afternoon when Roy heard about the murders over the radio while waiting for an order of French fries with gravy at the take-out window of The Cottage. Marvin Fish, who had dropped out of school the year before at the age of sixteen, having not gotten past the eighth grade, was working the window.

"Jesus on a pony," said Marvin, when he heard the news. "I ain't lettin' my little sister outta the house alone no more."

"The Grimes sisters weren't alone," Roy said. "They were with each other."

"Wait a second."

Marvin Fish turned up the volume on an oil-spattered Philco portable that was on a shelf above the deep fryer.

"The sisters were reported missing on March fifteenth, three weeks ago," said the man on the radio, "one day after they did not return home after school."

"Nobody woulda never reported me missin'," said Marvin. "I didn't used to go home after school, which I hardly ever went to anyway."

"Authorities believe that the girls were kidnapped," the radio voice reported, "then driven to the woods, where they were assaulted and killed. Their decomposing bodies were discovered by a transient who apparently stumbled over the shallow graves. The transient, whose name was not released, is being held as a suspect. Police say he may have committed the murders and for some reason returned to the scene of the crime."

"What's a transit?" asked Marvin Fish.

"Transient, a bum," said Spud Ganos, who with his wife, Ida, owned The Cottage. He had come out from the back and was standing next to the fryer. "Just another friggin' guy tryin' the wrong way to get the bad taste of the world out of his mouth."

"Here's your fries," Marvin said to Roy, "with extra gravy. No charge for the extra gravy."

Roy put seven nickels on the counter.

"Thanks, Marvin," he said, and picked up the soggy bag. "Where'd you get all the buffaloes?"

"Won 'em laggin' baseball cards."

"School ain't dismissed for two hours yet," Marvin said. "What're you doin' out?"

"Mrs. Murphy said the next time I was late she wouldn't let me into class. Told her I had to take a whiz was why I was late today, but she said I shoulda planned better and to take a hike."

"Murphy, yeah, I had her a couple times. Whenever there was a loud noise she'd say, 'Set 'em up in the other alley.'"

"Still does."

It was too early for Roy to go home, so he walked slowly toward the park, eating his fries with gravy. The rain had diminished to a cold drizzle. Roy had on a White Sox cap and a dark blue tanker jacket that according to the label was water repellent. He did not understand the difference between water proof and water repellent. Roy thought that they should mean the same thing but apparently they did not. Elephant or rhinoceros hides were water proof, he figured, like alligators and crocodiles, as opposed to swan, goose and duck feathers, which were merely water repellent. Ducks and geese flew sometimes, so perhaps that's how they dried off. Roy didn't remember if swans could fly or not.

When he got to the park, Roy perched on the top slat of a bench and looked at the muddy baseball field. What had happened to the Grimes sisters could happen to any kid, he decided, even if a kid didn't accept a ride in a car from a stranger. Someone who was bigger and stronger could grab a kid, or even two kids, especially if they were girls, and force them into a car.

The bottom of the bag was so wet from all the gravy that there was a hole in it. Roy had to keep one hand underneath the bag to keep the few remaining fries from falling out. The Grimes girls had been assaulted, the man on the radio said. Roy wondered if being assaulted and being molested were the same thing, or if there was some kind of difference, like between water proof and water repellent. It began raining harder again. Nobody would be playing ball today, that was for sure.

Johnny Across

Marcel Proust wrote, "One slowly grows indifferent to death." To one's own, perhaps, but not, Roy was discovering, to the deaths of others. Almost daily now, it seemed, certainly weekly, he heard or read of the death of someone he knew or used to know, however briefly, at some time during the course of his fifty-plus years. This, combined with the noticeable passing of various public persons who had made a particular impression upon him, had begun to affect him in a way he could not have predicted. What disturbed Roy most, of course, were the deaths of people he cared for or upon whom he looked favorably. The others—former adversaries, political despots or murderers languishing behind bars—had been as good as dead to him already. Early on in Roy's life he had developed a facility for excising certain people from his consciousness. He simply ceased to care about those individuals he felt were unworthy of his friendship and trust. He really did not care if they lived or died; what they did or did not do concerned him not at all.

During the winters when Roy attended grammar school in Chicago, the boys played a game called Johnny Across Tackle. Often upwards of thirty kids aged nine to thirteen would gather in the gravel schoolyard, which was covered with snow, during recess or lunch break or after classes were over, and decide who would be the first designated tackler. The rest of the boys would line up against the brick wall of the school building, a dirty brown edifice undoubtedly modeled after the factories of Victorian England, which was perhaps fifty feet long. This would be the width of the field. Sixty yards or so across the schoolyard was a chain link fence. The object was to run from the wall to the fence and back again as many times as possible without being tackled. The wall and the fence were "safe." Nobody could be tackled if they were touching with some part of their body—usually a hand, sometimes as little as a toe—the wall or the fence.

Somebody would volunteer to be "it," the first designated tackler. The object, of course, was to be the last man standing. They mostly played when there was a thick layer of snow over the gravel, to protect them from being cut by the stones. Even so, boys would be bruised and battered during this game; broken arms, wrists, ankles and fingers and the occasional broken leg were not uncommon. Girls would play a tag version of the same game, a more sensible exercise. Roy thought he should have taken this as an early sign that women were, if not superior, the more sensible sex.

The boy who was "it" would survey the lineup, pick out his quarry—usually one of the weaker kids, an easy target—and shout, "Johnny Across!" All of the Johnnys would then take off for the opposite safety of the fence. Each participant wanted to be the last survivor, the "winner," except that whoever won knew he would be piled on by however many of the tacklers as possible.

If the last boy was well-liked, the others would take him down tenderly, with respect for his toughness and athleticism. If, however, "Lonely Johnny," as Crazy Jimmy K., an older friend of Roy's who claimed to have achieved that distinction more than twenty times, called him, was unpopular with the majority of the rest of the players, the result could be decidedly ugly. Often, in order to avoid an animalistic conclusion, a kid who knew he was going to get it if he managed to make it through to the end would go down on purpose early in the game and get in his licks on the tackles.

When Roy was eleven years old, he was troubled by frequent nosebleeds. As his doctor explained, this was a not uncommon occurrence during rapid growth spurts. Blood vessels in Roy's nose would burst at any time, even when he wasn't exerting himself. One weekday morning in the middle of February, Roy went to the doctor's office to have his nose cauterized. The doctor inserted what looked to Roy like a soldering iron up each of his nostrils and burned the ends of the broken blood vessels. He then lubricated Roy's nasal passages, packed them with gauze, and instructed him to avoid contact sports for ten days. He handed Roy a tube of Vaseline and said he should not let his nostrils dry out, not blow his nose, and not pick at the scabs that would form, even if they itched. Then Roy took a bus to school.

Just as he arrived, the guys were gathering in the schoolyard to begin a game of Johnny Across. Roy ran over and joined them. The first designated tackler had already been chosen, Large Jensen, a Swedish kid who volunteered to start at tackle almost every time he played. Large, whose real name was Lars, was, at six feet tall and two hundred pounds, the biggest twelve year old on the Northwest side of the city. At least none of the kids at Roy's school had heard of or encountered anyone able to dispute this claim. Large said he had recently run into a kid at Eugene Field Park who was an inch taller and almost as heavy, but that kid was already thirteen, which Large would not be until June. Large's mother, whom the boys called Mrs. Large, had the widest hands Roy had ever seen on a woman. He was sure she could hold two basketballs in each one if she tried. Mrs. Large was wide all over but not very tall. Large's father—Mr. Large—was six feet six and probably weighed around 350. He worked over in Whiting or Gary, Indiana, for U.S. Steel. Large told the boys that as soon as he was sixteen he was going to quit school and go to work for U.S. Steel, too. His father already had a silver lunchbox with LARS stenciled on it in black block letters, just like his own, which was labeled OLAF.

Roy kept to the edges of the field, holding his head steady as he could and running at moderate speed. For some reason Roy thought that if he ran fast the intensity might disrupt the healing process. For a while, he was able to avoid any serious contact, and in particular kept away from Large Jensen and his mob. When Roy found himself one of only twelve remaining boys, he knew he had to either allow himself to be brought down without a struggle or risk serious damage.

On the next across, two of the tacklers, Thomas Palmer and Don Repulski, targeted Roy. Palmer was cross-eyed and couldn't tackle worth a damn. A straight arm would fend him off. Repulski worried Roy, however. He was bigger than Roy, six months older, a little fat but strong. Roy was faster, so he knew he had to make a good fake and hope Repulski would go for it, then Roy could beat both of them to the wall.

The rule was that the tacklers yelled "Johnny Across" three times. If a kid didn't move off the safe—the fence or the wall—after three calls, he was automatically caught. Roy waited through two calls, then, just as Palmer and Repulski started to shout "Johnny Across!" for the last time, he broke to his left, toward the eastern boundary of the schoolyard. This gave him more room to maneuver and would, perhaps, even enable him to outrun them to the boundary before he cut downfield toward the wall.

Roy slugged Thomas Palmer right between his crossed eyes with the flat of his right hand just as he reached the edge of the field. Palmer's glasses flew off and he went down on his knees. Roy didn't wait to see if he had made Palmer cry or if the busted frame had gashed his forehead. Roy had Repulski to beat, and as Roy made a hard cut his left foot gave way on the wet snow. Roy's left knee touched the ground and Don Repulski, unable to brake, barreled past him out of bounds. Roy recovered his balance and hightailed it to the wall. He was safe.

Palmer was yelling his head off. He claimed that Roy had gone down as a result of their contact. Roy's knee had hit the ground, Palmer said, so he was caught. Palmer had an inch-long cut on the bridge of his nose and was holding the two pieces that were his glasses. "No way!" Roy shouted. "I hit Palmer before I made my cut. He went down and then I turned—that's when my knee touched the snow." Repulski backed Roy up, he'd seen what happened. He started to say something else but then he—and everybody else—stopped talking. They were all just staring at Roy.

Roy had forgotten about his nose. He looked down and saw that the snow directly below him was turning bright red. Blood was streaming from both of his nostrils. He pulled the packet of tissues out of his coat pocket, tore it open, took a wad and jammed it up against his face. Blood soaked through the tissues in a few seconds, so he threw that wad away and made another. Slowly, the bleeding subsided. Holding a third bunch of tissues to his nose, Roy leaned back against the wall. He took out the tube of Vaseline, unscrewed the cap, squeezed ribbons of it up his nostrils and set himself for the next Johnny Across.

There were only four kids left on safe. Four against thirty. Repulski and about seven other guys stood directly in Roy's path. Palmer was not among them but Large Jensen was. At the second call, Roy took off, faked left, went right and banged against Large Jensen's stomach. Roy hit the ground hard and sat still. He glanced down without moving his head much; a few crimson drops dotted the snow. Large and the rest of the gang ran off to tackle someone else.

The school bell rang, signaling the end of the lunch break.

"Who's Lonely Johnny?" Roy asked Small Eddie Small.

"Nobody," he said, as he walked by. Roy got up and followed him. All four of the remaining Johnnys had been tackled before making it to the fence, the last two or three at about the same moment, so there was no winner. Repulski came trotting by and punched Roy's right shoulder.

"Good game," he said. Vaseline had congealed in Roy's throat. He hawked it up and expectorated a mixture of clotted blood and petroleum jelly, then walked into the building.

What Roy didn't realize until much later was that Johnny Across had been a valuable learning experience for life—and death. This business of living and dying, Roy concluded, was just one big game of Johnny Across, with everyone scampering to avoid being tackled. Back then, though, his biggest concern was how to stop his nose from bleeding. Ten days after Roy's nostrils were cauterized, he returned to the doctor to have him remove the scabs so that Roy could resume breathing properly. By this time Roy had swallowed enough Vaseline to have lubricated his mother's Oldsmobile for the next six months.

Roy had played Johnny Across several times during this "healing" period, and had luckily avoided direct contact involving his nose except for one sharp blow by Small Eddie Small's left elbow that engendered only a brief trickle. The guys, Roy thought, did not want to witness another vermilion snow painting, so they mostly took it easy on him. He took it easy on himself, too, but Roy knew, even then, that if he kept playing it safe, in the long run he would never become Lonely Johnny.

The Secret of Little White Dove

The morning after Thanksgiving, Roy went to meet the Viper and Jimmy Boyle on the corner of Blackhawk and Dupré. The weather was miserable; icy rain sputtered out of a dark gray sky but there was no school and the boys didn't want to spend any more time than they had to cooped up inside with their families.

Roy had the hood of his blue parka up and he wore the pair of oversized Air Force gloves his cousin Bink had given him the last time Bink had been home on leave. Roy loved these gloves. They were supposed to keep a pilot's hands warm even if the temperature dropped to fifty below. The gloves were silver-blue and shiny; they almost glowed in the dark. Roy didn't mind the lousy weather so much now that he could wear his Air Force gloves.

He saw Jimmy Boyle talking to Red Fellows, a washed up prizefighter in his late thirties who hung out at Beebs and Glen's Tavern. Roy had never seen Fellows box but the Viper said he'd heard Skull Dorfman tell Larry the Leg that Red had a left hook like his sister's and a right hand like his other sister's. Pops, Roy's grandfather, told him that Rocky Marciano had the best right hand in the business. "After his match with Marciano," Pops told Roy, "Joe Louis said, 'That boy don't fight by the book, but tonight I got hit by a library.'"

Roy arrived at the corner the same moment the Viper appeared from the opposite direction, just in time to see Red Fellows extract his left arm from his pea coat and roll up his shirtsleeve.

"See this?" he asked the boys.

On his biceps was a tattoo of a naked woman. Written under the legs were the words, "Little White Dove."

"I got it done in Germany," Red said, "when I was in the army. It's of a girl I met over there in a club in Berlin."

"Why does it say 'Little White Dove'?" asked Jimmy Boyle.

"I give her the nickname. Her actual name was Ingrid Meister."

"Why'd you call her that?"

Red Fellows grinned. The two teeth to the left of his only remaining front tooth were missing.

"It's what I called her most private part," he said. "Named it after the girl in the song, the Injun broad who fell in love with her brother."

Red rolled down his sleeve and put his arm back into his coat.

"You guys don't know what I'm talkin' about, do you?"

Nobody answered.

"Didn't think so. It's the secret to pleasin' a woman. She'll show you what to do with it but you gotta ask. Don't be afraid to ask."

Red Fellows walked away. Roy, Jimmy Boyle and the Viper, none of whom had yet turned twelve years old, stood under the black and orange-striped awning in front of Bompiani's Bakery and watched the rain turn to ice on the sidewalk.

"The name of the Indian girl's brother was Running Bear," said Roy. "That's the name of the song. Johnny Horton made the record."

"Red's a man of the world," Jimmy Boyle said.

"Where's he been other than Germany?" asked the Viper. "He never fought no further from Chicago than Fort Wayne."

"Red knows his way around," said Jimmy.

"He knows how to get to Beebs and Glen's," said Roy.

A hard wind swept water under the awning, soaking the boys' pants and shoes.

The Viper said, "Shit, at least Red knows enough to get in out of the rain."

That night on his way home, Roy cut through the alley behind Wabansia and Prairie. As he passed a passageway between two of the garages, Roy heard an eerie sound, some terrible combination of sobbing and snorting the way a horse does just after it stops running. Roy stopped and listened. The rain had quit a few hours before and the temperature had fallen. The surface of the alley was almost entirely iced over and glistened in the moonlight. Roy edged closer to the garage nearest him. The snorting noise became punctuated by a guttural sound, then ceased altogether. The sobbing lessened but continued.

A man walked out of the passageway. Roy flattened himself against the garage door. The man turned up the alley and walked in the direction from which Roy had come. He was average-sized and wore a short, dark jacket and a dockworker's cap. Roy heard another noise coming from the passageway, the sound of a person trying to stand up but slipping and falling in the attempt, scraping the wall with his body.

A second man came from the passageway. He stopped at the entrance to the alley and rubbed his face with both hands. When he dropped them, Roy could see that it was

Red Fellows. Red blinked his eyes hard a few times, then worked them over again with his fists. He seemed unsure of where he was or in which direction he should go. Roy knew that he did not want Red to see him, though he was not entirely certain why. Roy had witnessed nothing and he did not even know what it was he had heard. Still, he was afraid. If Red looked his way, Roy decided, he would run and hope Red did not recognize him.

Red put his right hand against the brick wall to his right and leaned on it. He coughed and brought up some phlegm, then spat it on the ground. Red leaned there for a few moments, then stood up straight, steadied himself, and began walking up the alley in the same direction the other man had gone.

Roy watched Red negotiate the slippery, cracked concrete with mincing steps, stopping several times as he made his way, until Red was out of sight. Roy then peeled himself off the garage door and headed toward his house. The sky was now so clear that he could plainly see the seven stars that formed either the Big Dipper or the Little Dipper. Roy was not sure if the constellation was Ursa Major or Ursa Minor, but he did remember that the scientific name of the North Star was Polaris.

The Delivery

I went up the stairs carrying the two shopping bags full of Chinese food figuring on a fifty-cent tip. It was a good Sunday due to the rain, people stayed in. I had two more deliveries in the bicycle basket. I rang the third-floor doorbell and waited, feeling the sub gum sauce leak on the bottom of one of the bags.

A woman opened the door and told me to please put the bags on the kitchen table, pointing the way. I put down the bags and looked at the woman. She was wearing a half-open pink nightgown, her nipples standing out against the thin material. Her hair was black halfway down her head, the bottom half was bleached and stringy.

"How much is it?" she asked.

"Five dollars," I said, looking at her purpled cheeks and chin.

"Just wait here and I'll get it for you," she told me. "Be right back."

I looked around the kitchen. I was twelve years old and was not used to being alone in strange kitchens. There were dishes in the sink, and one of the elements of the overhead fluorescent light was burned out, giving the kitchen a dull, rosy glow, like the woman's face, and her nightgown.

The woman came back and gave me a fifty-dollar bill. She

had put on a green nightgown similar to the one she'd had on before, and flicked her pink tongue back and forth through her purple lips.

"I don't have any change for this," I said. "Don't you have anything smaller?"

She smiled. "Well, I'll just go see!" she said, and went off again.

I sat down on the kitchen table. I was beginning to enjoy myself, and was disappointed when she returned in the same green nightgown. She handed me a twenty.

"Will this do?" she asked.

I dug in my pocket for the change but she stopped me.

"Don't bother, darling," she said, smiling, and put her hand on my wrist. Her nails were painted dark red, but looked lighter in the hazy glow. "Keep it all," she said, and took me by the hand to the front door.

She put my hand on her breast. I could feel a lump through the nightgown.

"Thank you very, very much," she said, heavily, like Lauren Bacall or Tallulah Bankhead. I thought she looked like Tallulah Bankhead except for her hair, which was more like Lauren Bacall's.

"You're welcome," I said, and she opened the door for me, letting me out.

It was still raining, but I stood for a minute under the Dutch elm tree where I'd left my bike and the bags of food covered by a small piece of canvas. I removed the cover from the bicycle and folded it over the bags in the basket. I felt the twenty-dollar bill in my pocket, and I smiled. If I could have two deliveries like this a day, I thought, just two.

The Deep Blue See

Whative When I was in the eighth grade I was given the job of being one of the two outdoor messengers of Clinton School. Since I was far from being among the best behaved students, I could only surmise that some farsighted teacher (of whom there were very few) realized that I was well suited for that certain responsibility, that perhaps some of my excess energy might be put to use and I'd be honored and even eventually behave better because of this show of faith in my ability to run errands during school hours. Either that or they were just glad to get rid of me for a half hour or so.

I thought it was great just because it occasionally allowed me to get out of not only the classroom but the school. Escorting sick kids home was the most common duty but my favorite was walking the blind piano tuner across California Avenue to and from the bus stop.

For two weeks out of the year the old blind piano tuner used to come each day and tune all of the pianos in the school. My job during that time was to be at the bus stop at eight forty-five every morning to pick him up, and then, at whatever time in the afternoon he was ready to leave, to walk him back across, wait with him until the bus arrived, and help him board.

We became quite friendly over the two-week period that

I assisted him. The piano tuner looked to me like any ordinary old guy with white hair in a frayed black overcoat, except he was blind and carried a cane. My dad and I had seen Van Johnson as a blind man in the movie *Twenty-three Paces to Baker Street*. Van Johnson had reduced an intruder to blindness by blanketing the windows and putting out the lights, trapping him—or her, as it turned out—until the cops came, but I'd never known anybody who was blind before.

I couldn't really imagine not being able to see and on the last day I asked the piano tuner if he could see anything at all. We were crossing the street and he looked up and said, "Oh yes, I see the blue. I can see the deep blue in the sky and the shadows of gray around the blue."

It was a bright sunny winter day and the sky was clear and very blue. I told him how blue it was, I didn't see any gray, and there were hardly any clouds. We were across the street and I could see the bus stopping a block away.

"Were you ever able to see?" I asked.

"Oh yes, shapes," he said. "I can see them move."

Then the bus came and I helped him up the steps and told the bus driver the old man was blind and to please wait until I'd helped him to a seat. After the piano tuner was seated I said good-bye, gave the token to the driver, and got off.

While I was waiting at the corner for the traffic to slow so that I could cross, I closed my eyes and tried to imagine what it was like to be blind. I looked up with my eyes closed. I couldn't see anything. I opened them up and ran across the street.

Radio Goldberg

Rigoberto Goldberg was a tall, lanky kid, an Ichabod Crane with thick glasses bordered by heavy black rims who didn't talk much. He also had a mustache, which no other twelve year old in Roy's neighborhood had. Dickie Cunningham thought it might have been because of Goldberg's being half Spanish.

"Puerto Rican kids grow up faster than we do," he said.

"Goldberg isn't from Puerto Rico," Roy told him. "He was born in the Dominican Republic."

"Where's that?"

"An island around Cuba, I think," said Roy. "And how do you know Spanish kids grow up faster? Mostly they're smaller than us."

"They're shorter," said Cunningham, "but they got hair on their chins when they're our age. Lookit that kid Luis went to Margaret Mary."

"One got thrown out for pullin' a switchblade on a teacher?"

Cunningham nodded. "Luis Soto somethin'."

"Sotomayor."

"Kid had a goatee in seventh grade."

"He was thirteen already. Got put back twice."

Rigoberto Goldberg was not an outstanding student. Once

in a while he'd crack wise in class, but mostly he seemed content to sit in the back row and hope to be ignored by the teacher. None of the other kids even knew if he could speak Spanish. Cunningham asked him if he could but Goldberg just shrugged and walked away. He was a real loner.

It was a surprise, therefore, when one afternoon after school Goldberg approached Roy and Cunningham and asked them if they wanted to see his radio station.

"What do you mean, your radio station?" asked Cunningham.

"I got a radio station," said Goldberg, "in my garage. I built it."

"Sure," Roy said. "Let's go."

As they walked to Rigoberto's house, Cunningham said, "Do you have call letters for your station, like WLS or WBBM?"

"I got a name," he told them. "Radio Goldberg."

"Wait a minute," said Roy, "don't you have to have letters? I thought east of the Mississippi River radio stations are all K-something, and west of the Mississippi they begin with W."

"It's my station," said Rigoberto. "I can call it whatever I want to."

Inside his family's garage, Goldberg had constructed what appeared to be a gigantic crystal set. He sat down in front of the table it was on, placed earphones over his head, switched on the machine and began turning dials. With his thick black glasses, droopy nose, uncombed dark brown hair and mustache, Goldberg looked every bit the mad scientist. All sorts of squealy, squeaky, dissonant noises emanated from the equipment, rattling off the brick walls. Several voices filled the room simultaneously. Roy felt as if he were inside a fun house at an amusement park. Rigoberto remained calm, fiddling the controls with his spiderleg fingers. For the first time, Roy noticed that Goldberg had an inordinate amount of dirt under his fingernails.

Suddenly, the cacophony ceased and Rigoberto spoke into a large, wood-framed microphone.

"Hey there, you with the stars in your eyes," he said, "this is Radio Goldberg, broadcasting from the forty story Goldberg Building located in the heart of the heartland, Chicago, Illinois, U.S. of A. Seven hot watts for all you guys, gals and tots."

Goldberg at the mike was an astounding sight to Roy and Cunningham. He transformed himself from a geeky, shirt-buttoned-up-to-the-collar, four-eyed bed-head into a smooth-talking ball of fire. Amazingly, Goldberg's body language became that of a slinky jungle cat's, and his voice had the timbre of Vaughan Monroe's recording of "Ghost Riders in the Sky." Rigoberto talked about whatever was on his mind at the moment. He trashed teachers of his by name, castigated girls he deemed stuck up because they wouldn't give him the time of day, and he played records. Goldberg owned only a few 45s; these included such diverse platters as Patti Page's "How Much is that Doggie in the Window?," Little Richard's "Good Golly, Miss Molly," and Jim Backus's spoken word rendering of the story of "Gerald McBoing Boing."

Radio Goldberg's broadcasting area, Rigoberto told Roy and Cunningham, encompassed approximately the six blocks surrounding his house. He came on the air after school on weekdays for a couple of hours, occasionally at night if his parents were out, and early Sunday mornings while his parents were still asleep. On Sunday, he said, he liked to tell his listeners that sometimes he thought he was a son of God, like Jesus, and then he would play Elvis Presley's record, "I

Believe." His parents, Rigoberto said, knew nothing about Radio Goldberg.

It wasn't long after he had revealed his secret station to Roy and Cunningham that Goldberg's neighbors began lodging complaints with the legitimate local radio stations whose signals were irregularly being interfered with. Three weeks into his broadcasting career, the police, armed with a search warrant, knocked on the Goldbergs' door. They discovered Rigoberto's garage set-up and confiscated his equipment. A small article describing the dismantling of Rigoberto Goldberg's operation appeared in the evening paper, the *Daily News*, under the heading, 'RADIO GOLDBERG' GOES OFF THE AIR. BOY, 12, CITED FOR BROADCASTING ILLEGALLY. The article quoted Arturo Goldberg, Rigoberto's father, who said, "My son is a genius. One day, you'll see."

"They fined me fifty bucks," Rigoberto told Roy and Cunningham. "My parents paid it but they're making me pay 'em back out of the money I earn from my paper route."

"Did the police return your equipment?" Roy asked him.

"Not yet. They still got my records, too."

"The cops are a bunch of crooks," said Cunningham. "One of 'em'll probably swipe 'Gerald McBoing Boing' and give it to his kid."

Why Skull Dorfman Went to Arkansas

Roy usually avoided Skull Dorfman's booth, but when Skull himself beckoned, Roy went over.

"Here, kid," Skull said, after reaching into one of his pants pockets and coming up with a five dollar bill, "get me a *Form* and an *American*." As Roy took the fin from him, Skull added, "Make that a *Sun-Times*, too. And don't forget to give the girl somethin'."

Roy walked to the front of Meschina's, where Flo, who'd been a blonde the last time Roy had seen her, was working the cash register.

"Hi, Flo," Roy said. "I like your hair."

Flo smiled, patted the back and sides of her head, and said, "Thanks, hon. I was a redhead once before, you know. I changed it to black after Tony Testonena and me went on the permanent outs. Feel like myself again. Ain't it late for you to be out, Roy? It's almost midnight."

"No, my mother doesn't care. She's probably not home yet, anyway. Can I have a *Racing Form*, an *American* and a *Sun-Times*, please? They're for Skull."

Roy handed Flo the five. He looked at her closely as she bent down to pick up the papers, put them on the counter, and then made change. Roy's mother was thirty-four years old and a real redhead. Flo had some serious creases in her face; cracks and crevices marred the thick, sand colored make-up around her eyes and mouth. His mother didn't have creases yet, at least none as evident as Flo's, and she didn't wear much make-up. Roy figured Flo had to be at least forty, if not older. She was skinny and her narrow breasts jutted out and up like steer horns. Cool Phil said they were falsies. Roy had only a vague idea of what falsies looked like. He wasn't crazy about Cool Phil because Phil was always in a bad mood and never had anything good to say about anybody. Roy thought maybe it was because Cool Phil, who was eighteen, six years older than Roy, had bad acne and was already losing his hair.

Flo gave Roy two dollars and fifty cents. "Here you go, hon," she said, and shot him a big smile. Her lips were thin, too, and she applied ruby red lipstick unevenly beyond the edges.

"Keep the quarters, Flo," said Roy, and handed them back to her. He folded the three papers under his right arm and kept the two singles in his left hand.

"Thanks, hon," Flo said, "you're a real gentleman."

Roy delivered the papers to Skull Dorfman, placing them carefully on the formica next to two empty and one half-eaten whitefish platters and a table barrel of old dills with three pickles left in it. He held out the singles toward Skull.

"I gave Flo four bits," Roy told him.

Seated across from Skull Dorfman in the booth was Arnie the Arm Mancanza. Arnie only had one arm, having lost his right in an industrial accident at Pocilga's sausage factory. The Arm carried a good three hundred pounds, and Dorfman had to go two-sixty or seventy, so Roy assumed the whitefish platters were merely a warm-up.

Skull plucked one of the bills from Roy's fingers and said, "The other one's yours, kid. I'm fat but I ain't cheap."

"You ain't fat, Skull," said the Arm. "I'm fat."

"Okay, Arm," Skull said. "Okay."

Roy joined his friends, who were occupying a booth in the back.

"How much he tip you?" asked the Viper.

"A buck."

"He pinch you on the cheek?" asked Jimmy Boyle. "I hate when he does that."

Roy shook his head no.

"He's a fat fuck," said the Viper.

"Arnie the Arm says Skull isn't fat," Roy said. "He says *he's* fat."

"Takes the Arm twice as long to eat since the accident at Pocilga's," said Jimmy Boyle. "His appetite ain't changed, just his velocity."

"What are you," the Viper said, "a fuckin' scientist?"

"My old man says Mancanza and Bruno Benzinger were feeding a stiff through the grinder is how it happened. Arnie got careless and caught his sleeve. By the time Benzinger turned off the machine, Mancanza's right arm was in slices."

"What happened to the stiff?" asked the Viper.

"Benzinger was a medic in Korea, so he tied a tourniquet onto what was left of Arnie's right arm to stop the bleedin', then finished off the stiff before takin' Mancanza to the hospital. My old man says if fuckin' Benzinger had taken the cut off parts of the arm, the doctors might have been able to reattach it, but he ground them up, too."

The next time Roy was in Meschina's, Skull Dorfman's booth was empty.

"Hey, Viper," Roy said, as he slid into a booth. "It's past midnight. Where's Skull?"

"You ain't heard what happened?"

"No."

"The Arm told Cool Phil Skull messed up. He got two jobs, you know, one tendin' a bridge on the river, the other as a parimutuel clerk at Sportsman's."

"Yeah, so?"

"You work for the city, you ain't supposed to work at the racetrack. It's a law."

"What happened?"

"Skull was at the track when he was supposed to be tending the bridge, and the fuckin' *Queen Mary* come through."

"The *Queen Mary* on the Chicago River?"

"One of them big god damn passenger liners. People want to see a river that flows backwards, I guess. Anyway, Skull's got his key on him, the one unlocks the switch raises the bridge. They're goin' nuts, nobody'll squeal on Skull, so the river pilot and the police don't know where he is. The *Queen Mary*'s bobbin' up and down, can't go nowhere. Everybody and their mother's pissed as hell. Takes 'em forever to find another key or break the lock. Finally, they get the bridge up. Skull gets back there, they put his ass in a sling."

"What did they do to him?"

"The Arm says Skull's suspended indefinitely from the bridge job without pay, and for sure he can't work the track no more unless he quits the city, which'd mean he'd forfeit his pension, which he got more'n twenty years in."

Jimmy Boyle came in and sat down next to Roy.

"I just told Roy about what happened to Skull," said the Viper.

"Yeah, the Arm's out front on the sidewalk," Jimmy Boyle said. "Heard him tellin' Oscar Meschina that Skull's in Hot Springs, workin' at a dog track."

"Where's Hot Springs?" the Viper asked.

"Arkansas," said Roy. "I was there once with my mother. Gambling's legal."

A couple came in and sat down in Skull Dorfman's booth.

"I guess it's true," said the Viper. "Don't look like Skull's comin' in."

Jimmy Boyle nodded. "Nope," he said, "not tonight, anyway."

Wanted Man

The summer I was thirteen years old I worked in Cocoa Beach, Florida, building roads and houses for my uncle's construction company. One afternoon when we were paving a street in one hundred and five degree heat, a police car pulled up to the site, stopped, and two cops got out, guns drawn. They moved swiftly toward the steam roller, which was being operated by Boo Ruffert, a former Georgia sheriff. The cops proceeded without a word and grabbed Boo, dragging him down from his perch atop the steam roller. I was shoveling limerock off of a curb directly across from the action, and I watched the cops handcuff Ruffert and begin double-timing him toward their beige and white. Jake Farkas, who had been sweeping behind Boo, jumped up onto the steam roller and shut it down before the machine went out of control and careened off the road. My uncle came running out of the trailer he used as an office and intercepted the policemen before they locked Boo Ruffert into the patrol car.

"Wait!" my uncle shouted at the cops. "What are you doing with him?"

"This man is wanted on a charge of child molestation in Georgia," said one of them. "We have a warrant for his arrest."

"Want to see it?" asked the other cop. He was holding the nose of his revolver against Ruffert's right temple.

"Listen," said my uncle, "Boo here is my best heavy equipment operator. He's almost finished with this street."

My uncle pulled out a roll of bills from one of his trouser pockets.

"Let me buy you fellows some lunch. Ruffert won't go anywhere, I'll keep an eye on him. You boys have something to eat while he finishes up here."

He held two fifties out toward them. "How about it?"

The cops looked at the money in my uncle's hand, then stuffed Ruffert into the back seat.

"Sorry," said one, "you'll have to get yourself another man. This one's headed to the hoosegow."

I had walked over and stood watching and listening to this exchange. I looked at Ruffert through the left side rear window. Boo grinned at me, exposing several brown teeth, and winked his right eye, the one with the heart-shaped blood spot on the lower outside corner of the white. I guessed Boo's age to be about forty. Jake Farkas came up and stood next to me. Jake always had the stub of a dead Indian, as he called cigars, in his mouth, usually a Crook, and three or four days' worth of whiskers on his face. He was in his early thirties but had already fathered, he told me, approximately thirteen children.

"You think you can ride her down the rest of the way?" my uncle asked Jake.

"Sure thing," Jake said.

My uncle turned and walked back to the trailer.

"Did you know about Boo?" I asked. "That he was a wanted man?"

Jake chuckled and said, "My dear old Mama used to say it's always good to be wanted, but I'm older now and I know that my dear old Mama weren't always right."

Jake strode to the steam roller, hopped up into the seat and cranked it over. I went back to shoveling limerock.

That evening, after my uncle dropped me off at a local movie theater while he went off to play cards, a bizarre incident occurred. I figured he was going to see a woman and that he knew I knew but seeing as how he had a wife in Miami, I assumed he thought it prudent not to tell me any more than he had to. I was not particularly fond of my aunt; my uncle knew this and most probably also knew I would never have betrayed his confidence had he chosen to tell me the truth, but this way neither of us had to compromise ourselves.

The movie was *Zulu*, which depicted red-jacketed, heavily-armed British soldiers in South Africa battling against Shaka's spear-throwing warriors. The theater was segregated; white patrons were seated downstairs and black patrons were seated in the balcony. This was in 1964, so some small progress had been made regarding racial equality in Florida in that both whites and blacks were at least allowed to be in the movie theater together.

The redcoats were vastly outnumbered by the Zulus, but their highly-disciplined British square defense—one line kneeling and firing as the line behind them stood and cleaned and reloaded their rifles—kept the natives at bay. The outcome, however, was inevitable; at some point the Zulus would overwhelm them. As the battle raged, there came from the balcony increasing shouts of exhortation directed at the Zulus, which incited equally fervent vocalizing by the white members of the audience below. The din inside the theater grew louder and more and more heated, practically drowning out the soundtrack of the picture.

Suddenly, the lights in the theater came on and the film stopped. The cinema manager jumped up onstage and stood in front of the screen. He was a large, mostly bald, clean-shaven white man wearing a baggy green suit. He held a lit cigarette between the second and third fingers of his right hand, the one he used to gesticulate and point toward the balcony. The crowd was silent.

"Listen up!" he shouted. "Any further ruckus and I'm throwin' all you niggers out of here!"

The manager kept his two cigarette fingers pointed at the balcony section for at least twenty seconds longer; then he put them to his mouth, took a long drag on the cigarette, exhaled smoke so that it curlicued slowly away from him and vanished in the lights, and dropped the butt to the floor where he ground it out with his right shoe. He did not lower his eyes from the cheap seats until he jumped down from the stage and unhurriedly proceeded up the center aisle and out into the lobby. The sound of the doors swinging shut was the only noise in the theater until the house lights blinked out and the projector resumed rolling.

The film ended with Shaka's Zulus acknowledging the bravery and ingenuity of the British regulars by saluting them and deciding against slaughtering them wholesale, thereby emerging victorious by having made the grandest and noblest heroic gesture possible before disappearing over a distant rise. I waited until almost every other patron had left the theater before I did. There was no trouble outside. The manager stood in front of the ticket booth, smoking. Up close, I could see several dark stains on the jacket and pants of his suit.

My uncle was parked in front of the theater. I climbed into his white Cadillac convertible and he drove away.

"How was the show?" he asked.

"Good," I said, "There was lots of fighting. Did you win?"

"Win?"

"Yeah, at the poker game."

"A little," said my uncle. "I always win a little."

We drove for a while without saying anything, then I asked, "What do you think will happen to Boo?"

"He'll do some hard time, I'm sure," my uncle said. "It's a bad business, messing with children."

"Was it a boy or a girl that he messed with?"

"A girl."

"How old was she?"

"Jake told me she was ten."

"How does he know?"

"What difference does it make? Ruffert was a wanted man, you won't ever see him again. Tell me more about the movie."

The Bucharest Prize

Roy was closing up the Red Hot Ranch, a hot dog shack where he worked three days a week after school and on Saturdays, when through the front window he saw a white Cadillac pull up to the curb. His mother got out of the passenger side. She was dressed to the nines, wearing a black cocktail dress beneath an ermine stole. Roy went outside to meet her. It was just after seven p.m., the sky was beginning to seriously darken and the air was cool.

"Roy, darling," said his mother, "I'm glad I caught you."

She bent a little to kiss him but barely brushed her maroon mouth against his left cheek so as not to smear her lipstick. Before Roy could say anything, she handed him a five dollar bill.

"This is for dinner, baby, and something extra," she said. "I won't be home until later tonight."

Roy looked at the car. A man he didn't know was seated behind the steering wheel. The man was wearing a midnight blue suitjacket over a tan shirt with a tie that matched his coat.

"Honey, you work so hard. Get some Chinese, the vegetables are good for you."

His mother's hair was flaming red, like Rita Hayworth's. She showed Roy every one of her spectacular teeth and waved goodbye to him as she got back into the Cadillac. The man had kept the motor running.

"Thanks, Ma!" Roy shouted as the car moved away.

Roy went back into the Ranch. He was thirteen years old and in a little more than an hour he would be playing in the city-wide All-Star baseball game. When he'd seen his mother arrive, he thought that she had come to take him to the ballpark, which was about half a mile away. He thought she had remembered his telling her the day before that he had been one of the youngest players chosen for the game; most of the All-Stars were fifteen or sixteen years old. She had never come to one of his games.

Roy did not start in the game that night but he got to pinch-hit in the sixth inning and he banged one off the lower right corner of the scoreboard for a triple, driving in two runs. Because he'd hit the scoreboard, Roy was awarded a case of Coca-Colas from the Bucharest Grocery.

After the game, knowing the case of Cokes would be too heavy to carry home, Roy passed the bottles out to the other players. They sat next to the field drinking Coca-Cola and talking about the game. The air had turned chilly but the boys were still perspiring and excited, so they joked and clowned around until they'd polished off most of the case.

Walking home, Roy felt sticky and cold from where sweat had dried underneath his wool uniform. He was proud to be seen wearing the shirt with the words All-Stars across the chest in big black letters. He hoped his mother would be home by now.

When Roy got there, the white Cadillac was parked in front of his house. He had one bottle of Coca-Cola left, stuffed in the left rear pocket of his baseball pants. Roy took it out and sat down on the steps of the Anderson house across the street. He'd given back the church key the boys had borrowed to open the other bottles to Marge Pavlik, the woman who ran the concession stand at the field. Roy had seen men take caps off bottles with their teeth but he didn't want to try it. Skip Ryan had lost part of his right front tooth that way; he could spit eight feet through the space.

Roy put down the bottle, closed his eyes, and thought about the ball he'd hit caroming off the scoreboard. It had rolled behind the rightfielder, who'd overrun it a little. After he'd slid into third base safely, Roy had stood up and looked back at the totals on the board, hoping the official scorer did not charge the outfielder with an error, which would have reduced the hit to a double. The Bucharest prize was given only for triples. No error was posted. The third base coach, Eustache "Stash" Pavlik, Marge's husband, had come over, said, "Good goin', kid," and swatted Roy on the behind.

Roy heard a car door open and close, followed by the sound of an engine starting. He opened his eyes and saw the white Cadillac disappearing around the corner. Roy stood up and headed across the street, then he remembered the Coke, went back and picked it up. Mrs. Anderson opened the front door.

"Roy," she said, "can I help you?"

"No, thanks, Mrs. Anderson. I was just sitting on your steps for a few minutes. I'm going home now."

"You look very nice in your uniform, Roy."

"Thanks."

"Did your team win?"

"Yes, ma'am, we did."

"Mr. Anderson and I like baseball. Tell us the next time you're going to play."

"I will, Mrs. Anderson."

Roy started to go, then he turned back.

"Mrs. Anderson, I won a case of Cokes tonight. Would you like one?"

He held the bottle out toward her. She took it.

"Thank you, Roy, how kind of you to offer. Good night."

"Good night," said Roy, "say hi to Mr. Anderson."

"I will."

Roy stood there.

"Roy," said Mrs. Anderson, "are you all right?"

Blows with Sticks Raining Hard

Roy wanted to get home before dark, so he decided to hitchhike rather than wait for a bus. At ten past five, when he left Little Louie's, the sky was gray with black stripes painted on the clouds. Snow began to fall as Roy stood in the slush next to the curb with his right thumb out.

He'd been sitting in the back booth at Louie's reading Joseph Conrad's *Congo Diary*, which he'd checked out of the Nortown branch library after having read *Heart of Darkness*. Roy had decided to write his next book report on *Heart of Darkness*, and his English teacher, Mr. Brown, had mentioned Conrad's *Congo Diary* as being interesting background material for the story. Roy enjoyed reading passages from Conrad's diary to his friends, especially to the girls, who hung out in Louie's after school.

"To Congo da Lemba after passing black rocks long ascent," Roy read to them. "Harou giving up. Bother. Camp bad. Water far. Dirty. At night Harou better."

After hearing this, Bitsy DiPena said, "Africa sounds icky. Why would anyone want to go there?"

"For jewels and ivory and minerals," Roy told her, "and slaves, of course."

"There's no slavery anymore, I don't think," said Susie

Worth, as she combed her long, blonde hair, which she did constantly. "Not in nineteen sixty-one."

"Arabs still have slaves," Jimmy Boyle said, "and some African tribes, too. I learned it in history."

"In the evening three women of whom one albino passed our camp," Roy read aloud. "Horrid chalky white with pink blotches. Red eyes. Red hair. Ugly. Mosquitos. At night when the moon rose heard shouts and drumming in distant villages. Passed a bad night."

"Spooky," said Susie Worth, biting on her comb.

"Spooky *and* icky," Bitsy DiPena said.

"Row between the carriers and a man about a mat. Blows with sticks raining hard."

"Stop it, Roy!" said Bitsy. "I don't want to hear any more."

It was getting colder as the light disappeared and snow came down harder. Roy kept his thumb out but nobody stopped. People were just off work, hurrying home or to the grocery stores. Roy began walking, turning every few steps to show drivers his thumb. Finally, a car pulled over, a dark green Plymouth sedan. It slowed, then idled a few yards ahead of Roy. He ran up to the Plymouth and opened the front passenger side door. The driver was a middle-aged man wearing an overcoat and a homburg hat. He had wire framed glasses and white hair.

"I'm going to Peterson," Roy said.

"Hop in," said the man. "That's in my direction."

Roy got into the car and pulled the door closed. The car heater was on full blast.

"Good to be out of this weather," the man said.

"Yeah, thanks," said Roy. "Didn't think anybody was going to stop."

"People are afraid to these days. You never know who you're picking up."

"I'm just a kid, though," said Roy.

"Even so," the man said, "you'd be surprised the things that happen."

Roy glanced again at the driver. He looked like he could be a minister. His face was bland, almost colorless.

"What's your name, son?"

"Roy."

"You go to high school?"

"Yes, sir. I'm a freshman."

"You're about fourteen, then."

"Almost."

"What are you interested in, Roy? What subjects?"

"Sports, mostly. I like to read, too."

"Good, good," the man said. "Are you reading a book now?"

"Yes. Joseph Conrad's *Congo Diary*."

"Really? That's impressive, Roy. Do you like it?"

"I like his descriptions of the people and places along the river where the boat stops. The crew walk inland sometimes and make camp. There's lots of insects and sickness. A boy gets shot. The boat has to avoid rocks that appear suddenly in the river. It's pretty exciting."

"You want to travel, Roy? Go to foreign places?"

"Uh huh. My uncle's been all over the world, he's always going somewhere. Right now he's in Mongolia. I'm going to be like him."

"What about the Bible, Roy? Do you read the good book? Are you a Christian?"

"My mother's a Catholic, but it doesn't interest me much. This is Peterson," said Roy. "You can let me out here."

"It's awfully bad outside," said the man. "What street do you live on? I can take you there."

"Rockwell, but you don't have to. I can walk over."

"It's only a couple of blocks out of my way. I'll take you."

The driver turned left on Peterson. The sky was completely black now.

"Where on Rockwell, Roy?"

"Near the corner," Roy said. "Here's okay."

The driver pulled the car over and stopped.

"You should go to church, Roy," he said. "You're a very bright boy. Christianity will help you to understand the mysteries of life."

The man placed his right hand firmly on Roy's left leg, up high, near his crotch. Roy yanked down hard on the handle of the passenger side door and got out of the car. He slammed it shut. The dark green Plymouth pulled away slowly, sliding through the snow, Roy thought, like a crocodile oozing off a Congo riverbank. He dropped his books and made a snowball, packing it hard with ice, then threw it at the car. The snowball hit the rear window, but the driver did not stop. Roy made another iceball. The Plymouth was almost out of sight. He didn't know where to throw it. Roy was not wearing gloves and his fingers were freezing. His eyes were tearing up from the wind. He hurled the snowball as far as he could across the street into the darkness.

"Night cold," Roy said out loud. "Natives hostile. Back to boat. Harou suffering again."

The Chinaman

I always spotted the Chinaman right off. He would be at the number two table playing nine ball with the Pole. Through the blue haze of Bebop's Pool Hall I could watch him massé the six into the far corner.

My buddy Magic Frank and I were regulars at Bebop's. Almost every day after school we hitched down Howard to Paulina and walked half a block past the Villa Girgenti and up the two flights of rickety stairs next to Talbot's Bar-B-Q. Bebop had once driven a school bus but had been fired for shooting craps with the kids. After that he bought the pool hall and had somebody hand out flyers at the school announcing the opening.

Bebop always wore a crumpled Cubs cap over his long, greasy hair. With his big beaky nose, heavy-lidded eyes, and slow, half-goofy, half-menacing way of speaking, especially to strangers, he resembled the maniacs portrayed in the movies by Timothy Carey. Bebop wasn't supposed to allow kids in the place, but I was the only one in there who followed the Cubs, and since Bebop was a fanatic Cub fan, he liked to have me around to complain about the team with.

The Chinaman always wore a gray fedora and sharkskin suit. Frank and I waited by the Coke machine for him to beat the Pole. The Pole always lost at nine ball. He liked to play one-pocket but none of the regulars would play anything but straight pool or nine ball or rotation. Sometimes the Pole would hit on a tourist for a game of eight ball but even then he'd usually lose, so Frank and I knew it wouldn't be long before we could approach the Chinaman.

When the Chinaman finished off the Pole he racked his cue, stuck the Pole's fin in his pocket, lit a cigarette, and walked to the head. Frank followed him in and put a dollar bill on the shelf under where there had once been a mirror and walked out again and stood by the door. When the Chinaman came out, Frank went back in.

I followed Frank past Bebop's counter down the stairs and into the parking lot next to the Villa Girgenti. We kicked some grimy snow out of the way and squatted down and lit up, then leaned back against the garage door as we smoked.

When we went back into the pool hall Bebop was on the phone, scratching furiously under the back of his Cub cap while threatening to kick somebody's head in, an easy thing to do over the phone. The Chinaman was sitting against the wall watching the Pole lose at eight ball. As we passed him on our way to the number nine table he nodded without moving his eyes.

"He's pretty cool," I said.

"He has to be," said Frank. "He's a Chinaman."

The End of Racism

One of my favorite places to go when I was a kid in Chicago was Riverview, the giant amusement park on the North Side. Riverview, which during the fifties was nick-named Polio Park, after the reigning communicable disease of the decade, had dozens of rides, including some of the fastest, most terrifying roller coasters ever designed. Among them were the Silver Streak, the Comet, the Wild Mouse, the Flying Turns, and the Bobs. Of these, the Flying Turns, a seatless ride that lasted all of thirty seconds or so and required the passengers in each car to recline consecutively on one another, was my favorite. The Turns did not operate on tracks but rather on a steeply banked, bobsledlike series of tortuous sliding curves that never failed to engender in me the sensation of being about to catapult out of the car over the stand of trees to the west of the parking lot. To a fairly manic kid, which I was, this was a big thrill, and I must have ridden the Flying Turns hundreds of times between the ages of seven and sixteen.

The Bobs, however, was the most frightening roller coaster in the park. Each year several people were injured or killed on that ride; usually when a kid attempted to prove his bravery by standing up in the car at the apex of the first long, slow climb, and was then flipped out of the car as it jerked suddenly downward at about a hundred miles per hour. The kids liked to speculate about how many lives the Bobs had taken over the years. I knew only one kid, Earl Weyerholz, who claimed to have stood up in his car at the top of the first hill more than once and lived to tell about it. I never doubted Earl Weyerholz because I once saw him put his arm up to the biceps into an aquarium containing two piranhas just to recover a quarter Bobby DiMarco had thrown into it and dared Earl to go after. Earl was eleven then. He died in 1958, at the age of fourteen, from the more than two hundred bee stings he sustained that year at summer camp in Wisconsin. How or why he got stung so often was never explained to me. I just assumed somebody had dared him to stick his arms into a few hives for a dollar or something.

Shoot the Chutes was also a popular Riverview ride. Passengers rode on boats that slid at terrific speeds into a pool and everybody got soaking wet. The Chutes never really appealed very much to me, though; I never saw the point of getting wet for no good reason. The Parachute was another one that did not thrill me. Being dropped to the ground from a great height while seated on a thin wooden plank with only a narrow metal bar to hold on to was not my idea of a good time. In fact, just the thought of it scared the hell out of me; I didn't even like to watch people do it. I don't think my not wanting to go on the Parachute meant that I was acrophobic, however, because I was extremely adept at scaling garage roofs by the drainpipes in the alleys and jumping from one roof to the next. The Parachute just seemed like a crazy thing to submit oneself to as did the Rotor, a circular contraption that spun around so fast that when the floor was removed riders were plastered to the walls by centrifugal force. Both the Parachute and the Rotor always had long lines of people waiting to be exquisitely tortured.

What my friends and I were most fond of at Riverview was Dunk the Nigger. At least that's what we called the concession where by throwing a baseball at a target on a handle and hitting it square you could cause the seat lever in the attached cage to release and plunge the man sitting on the perch into a tank of about five feet of water. All of the guys who worked in the cages were black, and they hated to see us coming. Between the ages of thirteen and sixteen my friends and I terrorized these guys. They were supposed to taunt the thrower, make fun of him or her, and try to keep them spending quarters for three balls. Most people who played this game were lucky to hit the target hard enough to dunk the clown one in every six tries; but my buddies and I became experts. We'd buy about ten dollars worth of baseballs and keep those guys going down, time after time.

Of course they hated us with a passion. "Don't you little motherfuckers have somewhere else to go?" they'd yell. "Goddamn motherfuckin' whiteboy, I'm gon' get yo' ass when I gets my break!" We'd just laugh and keep pegging hardballs at the trip-lever targets. My pal Big Steve was great at Dunk the Nigger; he was our true ace because he threw the hardest and his arm never got tired. "You fat ofay sumbitch!" one of the black guys would shout at Big Steve as he dunked him for the fifth pitch in a row. "Stop complaining," Steve would yell back at him. "You're getting a free bath, aren't ya?"

None of us thought too much about the fact that the job of taunt-and-dunk was about half a cut above being a carnival geek and a full cut below working at a car wash. It never occurred to us, more than a quarter of a century ago, why it was all of the guys on the perches were black, or that we were racists. Unwitting racists, perhaps; after all, we were kids, ignorant and foolish products of White Chicago during the fifties.

One summer afternoon in 1963, the year I turned sixteen, my friends and I arrived at Riverview and headed straight for Dunk the Nigger. We were shocked to see a white guy sitting on a perch in one of the cages. Nobody said anything but we all stared at him. Big Steve bought some balls and began hurling them at one of the black guys' targets. "What's the matter, gray?" the guy shouted at Steve. "Don't want to pick on one of your own?"

I don't remember whether or not I bought any balls that day, but I do know it was the last time I went to the concession. In fact, that was one of the last times I patronized Riverview, since I left Chicago early the following year and Riverview was torn down not long after. I don't know what Big Steve or any of my other old friends who played Dunk the Nigger with me think about it now, or even if they've ever thought about it at all. That's just the way things were.

Way Down in Egypt Land

There was a one-legged pool hustler named The Pharaoh who used to eat his dinner every day at four o'clock in a diner under the el tracks on Blackhawk Avenue called The Pantry. The neighborhood kids didn't know his real name, he just went by The Pharaoh because he said he came from Cairo, the tail of Little Egypt between the Mississippi and Ohio rivers.

"It's the asshole of Illinois," The Pharaoh told Roy and his friends, none of whom had ever been there.

"My mother had a cousin named Phil Webster was murdered in a bar in Paducah," said Ralph McGirr. "That's near there, ain't it?"

"Paducah's in Kentucky," The Viper said, "across the Ohio. It's pretty close."

The Pharaoh said nothing, just finished his meatloaf and mashed potatoes and dug into a slice of blueberry pie. The boys sat on stools in The Pantry or stood around, waiting for The Pharaoh to be done with his meal so that they could follow him down the street to Lucky's El Paso and watch him shoot pool. The El Paso was an old poolhall that had been closed down for years until Lucky Schmidt took it over. He renamed it Lucky's but everybody around there still called it the El Paso, so he changed it to Lucky's El Paso to pacify the old-timers. The Pharaoh didn't care what the place was called as long as it had a five by ten foot table to play one-pocket on. The Pharaoh always dressed the same: he wore a red and black checkered flannel shirt buttoned up to the neck and dark gray trousers held up by black suspenders. Once Roy had seen what looked like part of a thick blue scar below The Pharaoh's Adam's apple; Roy guessed that was why he kept his shirt buttoned to the top.

After The Pharaoh had polished off the pie, he propped himself up on his crutches and swung out of The Pantry. Jimmy Boyle held open the door and The Pharaoh turned right, followed by six boys aged twelve to fifteen. He didn't wear a coat. Nobody knew exactly how old The Pharaoh was or how he lost his left leg. Roy figured The Pharaoh was around forty or fifty years old because his curly brown hair was thinning and his forehead and cheeks were pretty wrinkled. The Viper said he'd heard Lucky ask The Pharaoh about how his leg went missing. This was while The Pharaoh was sitting down waiting for Ike the Kike to miss and without looking at Lucky The Pharaoh told him maybe someday he'd tell him but first Lucky should go fuck himself and his sister. After that, said The Pharaoh, they could talk about it.

The Pharaoh did not use his crutches when he shot; he supported himself by balancing his weight between his right leg and the table. The boys closely studied every move The Pharaoh made. His practice routine never varied: he lined up four balls at one end of the felt, hit them one after the other only just hard enough off the rail so that they came back to exactly the same spot at which he'd placed them. The Pharaoh did this three times with each ball unfailingly, then he was ready to play. Roy and his friends tried to emulate

The Pharaoh's warm-up but none of them could do it right more than once or twice. The only advice The Pharaoh would offer anyone was to tell them to tap the ball as if they were kissing their dead mother in her coffin.

The Pharaoh preferred one-pocket but occasionally indulged someone at nine ball. He never played straight pool, which he said was for stiffs. "If I'd bought into boredom," he told Roy, "I'd have stayed in school."

The only time Roy ever saw The Pharaoh lose was the last time he saw him, on a February night when he and The Viper went together to Lucky's El Paso. The boys came in out of the beginning of a blizzard around nine o'clock and saw a very tall, skinny guy bent low over the match table, the one Lucky kept covered even when the place was full of customers. The other tables he sometimes let bums sleep on after closing but not this one. There were about fifteen men sitting or standing in close proximity to the match table, watching this tower of bones beating the bejesus out of The Pharaoh at his own game. The Pharaoh sat perfectly still in the ratty red armchair he always used, his lone leg stretched out in front of him, an inch and a half of white cotton sock exposed between his trouser cuff and a beat up brown brogan. He was smoking an unfiltered Old Gold, staring at his imperturbable opponent.

The tall, skinny guy was about the same age as The Pharaoh but he was better dressed. He wore a dark blue blazer over an open-necked pale yellow shirt and chino pants. His few strands of black hair were greased back on his skull. Everything about him was long: his fingers, nose, even his eyelashes. Nobody spoke. Roy and The Viper stood and watched what were the final moments of the match, and when it was over the other witnesses to the slaying of The Pharaoh dropped their cash on the table and marched out of the poolhall into the storm.

The victor picked up his winnings, folded the bills into a thick roll, wrapped a blue rubber band around it and stuffed it into a pants pocket. Then he went over to The Pharaoh and said softly, but not so softly that Roy and The Viper could not hear the words, "You're washed up in Chi, Freddie, and don't never go back to Cairo, neither."

The Pharaoh sat and let his Old Gold smolder while the thin man unscrewed his cue, packed it into his case, pulled on a shabby beige trenchcoat, shook loose a Chesterfield from its pack to his lips, lit it, and without looking back at The Pharaoh left the El Paso. Lucky was sweeping up butts and putting the folding chairs away. He did not speak to The Pharaoh, nor did the boys, though they stood and waited for him. Roy thought maybe he'd need help walking in the snow.

After a half hour, The Viper elbowed Roy and they headed for the door. Before facing the blizzard Roy stopped and glanced over at The Pharaoh.

"Come on," said The Viper, "I'm hungry. Let's get some Chinks."

"Think he can make it to his crib?" Roy asked. "Where do you think he'll go?"

"I don't know," said The Viper, "but it probably won't be Little Egypt."

Bad Things Wrong

Louie Pinna was a bad kid, everybody said so: his neighbors, relatives, teachers. He was a bad student, that was certain. Pinna never really learned to read or write, so he was stuck in the third grade until he quit school legally at the age of sixteen. Roy had been in that third grade class with Pinna, a situation that was embarrassing not only for Louie but for his classmates, as well. At fifteen Pinna was already six feet tall. His legs did not fit under the small desk he was assigned to, so he sat in the last seat of the last row and splayed his legs to either side. Everyone was relieved when Pinna was finally allowed to leave.

After that Pinna hung out on the corner of Diversey and Blackhawk in the afternoons and worked as a night janitor at a downtown office building. Roy and his friends would often stop and talk to him after they got out of school. Pinna had always been nice to them; Roy never understood why so many adults considered Louie Pinna to be a rotten apple. In the 1950s, the concept of learning disabilities was not widely discussed, so a kid like Pinna was considered dumb and labelled a loser, earmarked for a bleak future as a bum or a criminal.

By the time Roy was in high school, Pinna had disappeared from the neighborhood. Roy asked around about him but nobody he talked to seemed to know where Pinna had gone. Then one day when Roy was fifteen Pinna's face appeared on the front page of the Chicago *Tribune*. Under a photograph of the now twenty-three year old Louie Pinna, who had grown a fruit peddler mustache, were the words: NO BAIL FOR SUSPECT IN KILLINGS. The article accompanying the photo said that Pinna worked at a meat processing plant on the West Side of the city and was accused of feeding bodies of murder victims through a grinder, after which the remains were mixed with food products and packaged as pork sausage. Pinna had not actually been charged with committing any murders, only with disposing of corpses provided, investigators theorized, by The Outfit, Chicago's organized crime syndicate.

Alberto Pinna, Louie's father, a retired plumber, was quoted in the newspaper as saying that his son had "a slow brain," and that, "if Louie done such a thing, he was used by those type people who do bad things wrong." Louie's mother, Maria Cecilia, was quoted as following her husband's statement with the remark, "And there ain't no short-age of them in Chicago."

"You believe this?" Roy asked the Viper.

"Pinna goes to prison," the Viper said, "at least he won't have to worry about taking care of himself no more."

"Do you think he did it? Ground bodies up for the Mob?"

"What makes you think he wouldn't?"

Roy and the Viper were on a bus passing the lake, which was frozen over. Roy remembered seeing Louie Pinna with Jump Garcia and Terry the Whip, both of whom had done time in the reformatory at St. Charles, going into Rizzo and Phil's, a bar on Ravenswood Avenue, a couple of years before. The cuffs of Pinna's trousers came down only to the tops of his ankles and he was wearing white socks with badly scuffed brown shoes. Rizzo and Phil's, Roy had heard, was supposedly a hangout for Mob guys.

"Pinna never picked on younger kids," Roy said. "He wasn't a bully."

"He did the thing," said the Viper, "ain't no character witnesses from grammar school gonna do him no good."

"Can't see what good it'd do to put Pinna away. He didn't harm a living person."

That night, Roy's mother's husband, her third, a jazz drummer who used the name Sid "Spanky" Wade—his real name was Czeslaw Wanchovsky—almost drowned in the bathtub. He had been smoking marijuana, fallen asleep and gone under. Spanky woke up just in time to regurgitate the water he'd inhaled through his nostrils. Roy's mother heard him splashing and coughing, went into the bathroom and tried to pull Spanky out of the tub, but he was too heavy for her to lift by herself.

"Roy!" she yelled. "Come help me!"

Roy and his mother managed to drag Spanky over the side and onto the floor, where he lay puking and gagging. Roy saw the remains of the reefer floating in the tub. Spanky was short and stout. Lying there on the bathroom floor, to Roy he resembled a big red hog, the kind of animal Louie Pinna had shoved into an industrial sausage maker. Roy began to laugh. He tried to stop but he could not. His mother shouted at him. Roy looked at her. She kept shouting. Suddenly, he could no longer hear or see anything.

Detente at the Flying Horse

Roy had a job changing tires and pumping gas two days a week after school at the Flying Horse service station on the corner of Peterson and Western. This was during the winter when he was sixteen. The three other weekday afternoons and also on Saturdays he worked at the Red Hot Ranch, a hot dog and hamburger joint. Roy had taken the gas station job in addition to his long-standing employment at the Ranch because his mother had had her hours reduced as a receptionist at Winnemac Hospital. His sister had just begun grammar school and they needed the money. Roy knew that his mother was considering getting married again—for what would be the fourth time—as a way to support them, a move he wanted desperately to avert or, at the least, delay. None of his mother's marriages had been successful, as even she would admit, other than two of them having produced Roy and his little sister. They were her treasures, she assured them; their existence had made her otherwise unfortunate forays into matrimony worthwhile.

Domingo and Damaso Parlanchín, two Puerto Rican brothers, owned the Flying Horse. They were good mechanics, originally from San Juan, who had worked for other people for fifteen years and saved their money so that they could buy their own station. They were short, chubby, good-humored men in their forties, constantly chattering to each other in rapid Spanish. The Parlanchín brothers paid Roy a dollar an hour and fifty cents for each tire he changed, half of what it cost the customer. Damaso could patch a flat faster than Roy could get it off the car and back on again, and do it without missing a beat in the running conversation with his brother. Domingo was the better mechanic of the two, the more analytically adept. Damaso was superior at handling the customers, able to convince them they needed an oil change or an upgrade of their tires.

It was no fun changing tires in January in Chicago. The temperature often fell well below zero degrees Fahrenheit and icy winds off the lake scorched Roy's perpetually scraped knuckles and cut fingers. Prying loose frozen lug nuts was Roy's greatest difficulty until Domingo showed him how to use an acetylene torch to heat the bolts before attempting to turn them with a tire iron. "Cuidado con la lanzallamas," Domingo told Roy.

One snowy afternoon about a quarter to four, just before dark, a black and white Buick Century ka-bumped into the station on its rims and stopped. All four tires were flat. Roy could see that they were studded with nails. Two burly men in dark blue overcoats and Homburg hats sat in the front seat. They did not get out, so Roy went over to the driver's side window and nodded at him. The man rolled down the window. He was about forty-five years old, had a three-day beard and a four inch-long scar across the left side of his lips. The man in the passenger seat looked just like the driver, except for the scar.

"How fast fix?" asked the driver.

"It looks like you need four new tires, sir," said Roy.

"Not possible fix?"

"I'll ask my boss, but I doubt it. You're riding on your rims. We'll have to check if they're bent."

"Go ask boss."

Roy trudged through the thick, wet snow to the garage, where Domingo and Damaso were working over a transmission on a 1956 Ford Apache pick-up.

"There's a guy here who needs four tires replaced. Looks like he drove over a bed of nails."

"Tell him he can to leave it," said Damaso.

"And coming back at siete horas," Domingo added.

The wind ripped into Roy's face when he removed his muffler from around his mouth to convey this information to the driver of the Buick. Roy's eyes stung; they watered as he waited for the man to respond.

"Cannot they fix now?"

"No," said Roy, "we're pretty backed up."

The driver spoke to his companion in a language Roy could not readily identify. The wind whined and shrieked, making it difficult for Roy to hear anything else.

"We wait," the driver told him. "Can fix sooner."

Roy shook his head. "Maybe you'd better try another station. But you'll damage your wheels."

The man produced a fifty dollar bill and shoved it at Roy. He held it between two black leather-gloved fingers. "This extra. Okey dokey?" he said. "You give boss."

Roy accepted the bill, marched back to the garage and handed it to Domingo.

"The guy says this is on top of the cost of replacing the tires, if we can do it now."

"Tell him drive in muy despacio," said Domingo.

After the man had done this, following Damaso's signals

to pull up into the other bay and onto the lift, Damaso told the men to get out of the car.

"We stay in," said the driver.

"No es posible raise car with you inside. Insurance no good if you fall."

The driver held out another fifty. Damaso took it. He nodded to Domingo, who activated the lift.

"Lock doors!" Damaso shouted up at the men. "And no move!"

Roy pumped gas for several customers while the Parlanchín brothers worked on the Buick. The sky had gone dark and snow kept falling. Before the Buick pulled out of the station on four new Bridgestones, it stopped next to Roy. The driver rolled down his window.

"Yes, sir?" said Roy. "Is everything okay?"

"All okey dokey," replied the driver. "You young boy, work hard bad weather. How much Spanish men pay you?"

"Buck an hour and two bits a flat."

"Slave wage," said the man. "Now 1962. Take."

The driver extended toward Roy his black gloved left hand between two fingers of which protruded another fifty-dollar bill. Roy took the money and stuffed it into one of the snap pockets of his brown leather jacket.

"Thank you," he said. "Where are you guys from?"

"You know Iron Curtain?"

"I've heard of it."

"We are from behind."

After the Buick had gone, Roy went into the garage.

"Strange hombres, si?" said Domingo.

"The driver gave me a tip," Roy told him. "I don't know why, though."

"He give us a hundred extra," said Damaso.

"The Buick had diplomatic license plates," Roy said. "They're Russians, I think."

"Must be they are trying to be more friendly," Domingo suggested, "since they been forced to take missiles out of Cuba."

When Roy was eleven, he remembered, his mother had had a boyfriend from Havana, a conga drummer named Raul Repilado. She had met him in Coral Gables, Florida, when she and her third husband, Sid Wade, the father of Roy's sister, were vacationing at the Biltmore. Raul Repilado's band, the Orquesta Furioso, was appearing at the hotel. Raul had come to Chicago a couple of times to see Roy's mother, the last time during the winter. Before leaving, the conguero declared that he would never come back to such a terribly cold place, even for a beautiful woman. Roy couldn't wait to tell his mother that he'd made an extra fifty bucks that day.

Shattered

Roy was walking to his after school job at the Red Hot Ranch when a girl about his age, whom he did not know, came up to him and said, "Isn't it terrible? I just want to scream."

Roy looked at her face. The girl was crying but she was still pretty. She had blonde hair and gray eyes. At closer inspection, Roy realized that the girl was older than he'd first thought; she was about eighteen or nineteen.

"Isn't what terrible?" he asked.

"You didn't hear?"

"I don't know," said Roy. "Hear what?"

"The president's been shot. He's dead."

Fresh tears shot out of the girl's eyes and poured down her cheeks.

"Can you hold me?" she asked him. "I need to be held, just for a few seconds."

Even though he was two or three years younger than the girl, Roy was at least two inches taller. He put his arms around her. She sank her head into his chest and continued sobbing.

"I'm shattered," she said. "I never imagined anything so terrible could happen."

"Do they know who shot him?"

The girl moved her head side to side without taking it off of Roy's chest.

"A woman shouted it from the window of a bus."

"Maybe the woman was crazy," Roy said. "Maybe it didn't happen at all."

"No, it happened. I've been walking for blocks and blocks and other people said it, too."

The girl remained in Roy's embrace for about a minute before she pulled away and wiped her face with the end of her scarf. It was a windy, cold day; the sky was overcast. Roy could feel snow in the air.

"Thank you," the girl said. Her gray eyes were bloodshot. "This is the worst thing that ever happened to me."

Later that night, after Roy had gotten home from work and watched the news on television, he thought about what the girl had said, that the assassination of the president was the worst thing that had ever happened to her, even though she was not the person who had been murdered.

When things go wrong, Roy decided, people are shocked by the discovery of their own lack of control over events. Perhaps now the girl would understand just how fragile the appearance of order in the world really was. All Roy wanted to think about was how pretty she was and how good it felt to hold her.

A Day's Worth of Beauty

The most beautiful girl I ever saw was Princessa Paris, when she was seventeen and a half years old. I was almost seventeen when I met her. An older guy I knew from the neighborhood, Gus Argo, introduced me to Princessa— actually, she introduced herself, but Gus got me there— because he had a crush on her older sister, Turquoise, who was twenty-two. This was February of 1963, in Chicago. The street and sidewalks were coated with ice, a crust of hard, two day-old snow covered the lawns. Princessa attended a different high school than I did, but I had heard of the Paris sisters; their beauty was legendary on the Northwest side of the city.

Argo picked me up while I was walking home from the Red Hot Ranch, a diner I worked at four days a week, three after-noons after school and Saturdays. It was about eight o'clock when Gus spotted me hiking on Western Avenue. He was twenty-one and had worked at Allied Radio on Western for three years, ever since he'd graduated from high school. Argo had been a pretty good left-handed pitcher, I'd played ball with and against him a few times; he was a tough kid, and he had once backed me up in a fight. A gray and black Dodge Lancer pulled over to the curb and honked. I saw that the driver was Gus Argo, and I got in.

"Hey, Roy, where you headed?"

"Thanks, Gus, it's freezing. To my house, I guess. I just got off work."

"Yeah, me, too, but I got to make a delivery first, drop off a hi-fi. Want to ride over with me? Won't take long."

"Sure."

"Your old lady got dinner waitin'?"

"No, she's out."

"Okay, maybe we'll get a burger and coffee at Buffalo's. I just got paid, so it's on me."

"Sounds good."

"Ever hear of the Paris sisters?"

"Yeah, everybody has. You know them?"

"I'm makin' the delivery to their house. I been tryin' to get up the nerve to ask Turquoise Paris to go out with me for two years."

"Are they really so good looking?"

"I'd give anything to spend one day with Turquoise, to have one day's worth of her beauty."

"What about the other one?"

"Princessa? She's almost eighteen, four years younger than Turquoise. I only saw her once, at the Granada on a Saturday. She's a knockout, too."

Gus cranked up the blower in the Dodge. The sky was clear black but the temperature was almost zero. The radiator in my room didn't work very well; I knew I would have to sleep with a couple of sweaters on to stay warm. Argo parked in front of the Paris house and got out.

"Come in with me," he said. "You can carry one of the boxes."

Princessa opened the front door. She was almost my

height, slender and small-breasted. Her lustrous chestnut hair hung practically to her waist. Once I was inside, in the light, I took a good look at her face. She reminded me of Hedy Lamarr in *Algiers*, wearing an expression that warned a man: If you don't take care of me, someone else certainly will. Princessa's complexion was porcelain smooth; I'd never before seen skin that looked so clean.

"You can just leave the boxes on the floor in the living room," she told us. "My father will set it up when he gets home."

"Who's there, Cessa?"

Gus Argo and I looked up in the direction from which the voice asking this question had come. Gene Tierney stood at the top of the staircase. Or maybe it was Helen of Troy.

"The delivery boys," Princessa answered. "They brought the new hi-fi."

"Tell them to just leave the boxes in the living room. Daddy will set it up later."

"I just did."

The apparition on the staircase disappeared; she wasn't coming down.

"Thanks, guys," said Princessa. "I'd give you a tip but I don't have any money. I can ask Turquoise if she does."

"No," Gus said, "it's okay."

He glanced at the top of the stairs once more, then walked out of the house.

"My name is Roy," I said to Princessa.

"Hi, Roy." she said, and held her right hand out to me. "I'm Cessa."

I took her hand. It felt like a very small, freshly killed and skinned animal.

"Your hand is warm," I said, holding it.

"My body temperature is always slightly above normal. The doctor says people's temperatures vary."

"It feels good. Mine is cold. I wasn't wearing any gloves." She withdrew her hand.

"Could I come back to see you sometime?" I asked.

Princessa smiled. Hedy Lamarr vanished. Princessa had one slightly crooked upper front tooth the sight of which made me want to kiss her. I smiled back, memorizing her face.

"It was nice to meet you," I said, and turned to go.

"Roy?"

I turned around. Hedy was back.

"You can call me, if you like. My last name is Paris. I have my own phone, the number's in the book."

I went out with Princessa a couple of times. She talked about her boyfriend, who was already in college; and about Turquoise, who, Cessa told me, was a party girl.

"What's a party girl?" I asked.

"She gets fifty dollars when she goes to the powder room, sometimes more. My parents don't know."

I didn't ask any more questions about Turquoise, but I did repeat what Princessa told me to Gus Argo.

"Fifty bucks for the powder room? You're shittin' me," he said.

"Does that mean she's a prostitute?" I asked him.

"I don't think so," said Argo. "More like she goes out with visiting firemen who want a good lookin' date."

"Visiting firemen?"

"Yeah, guys from out of town. Salesmen, conventioneers."

Many years later, I read Apuleius's version of the myth of

Psyche and Amor. Venus, Amor's mother, was so jealous of her son's love for Psyche that she attempted to seduce Amor in an effort to convince him to destroy his lover, which he would not do. Venus even imprisoned Amor and ordered Psyche to go to the underworld and bring up a casket filled with a day's worth of beauty. Eventually, Jupiter, Amor's father, came to his son's rescue and persuaded Venus to lay off the poor girl.

I remembered Gus Argo telling me he would have done anything to have had one day's worth of Turquoise Paris's beauty. My guess is that he never got it, and I doubt that he knew the story of Psyche and Amor. Gus just didn't seem to me like the kind of guy who'd spring for the powder room.

The Peterson Fire

It was snowing the night the Peterson house burned down. Bud Peterson was seventeen then, two years older than me. Bud got out alive because his room was on the ground floor in the rear of the house. His two sisters and their parents slept upstairs, above the living room, which was where the fire started. An ember jumped from the fireplace and ignited the carpet. Bud's parents and his ten and twelve year old sisters could not get down the staircase. When they tried to go back up, they were trapped and burned alive. There was nothing Bud Peterson could have done to save any of them. He was lucky, a fireman said, to have survived by crawling out his bedroom window.

I didn't see the house until the next afternoon. Snow flurries mixed with the ashes. Most of the structure was gone, only part of the first floor remained, and the chimney. I was surprised to see Bud Peterson standing in the street with his pals, staring at the ruins. Bud was a tall, thin boy, with almost colorless hair. He wore a Navy pea coat but no hat. Black ash was swirling around and some of it had fallen on his head. Nobody was saying much. There were about twenty of us, kids from the neighborhood, standing on the sidewalk or in the street, looking at what was left of the Peterson house.

I had walked over by myself after school to see it. Big

Frank had told me about the fire in Cap's that morning when we were buying Bismarcks. Frank's brother, Otto, was a fireman. Frank said Otto had awakened him at five-thirty and asked if Frank knew Bud Peterson. Frank told him he did and Otto said, "His house burned down last night. Everybody but him is dead."

I heard somebody laugh. A couple of Bud's friends were whispering to each other and trying not to laugh but one of them couldn't help himself. I looked at Peterson but he didn't seem to mind. I remembered that he was a little goofy, maybe not too bright, but a good guy. He always seemed like one of those kids who just went along with the gang, who never really stood out. A bigger kid I didn't know came up to Bud and patted him on the left shoulder, then said something I couldn't hear. Peterson smiled a little and nodded his head. Snow started to come down harder. I put up the hood of my coat. We all just kept looking at the burned down house.

A black and white drove up and we moved aside. It stopped and a cop got out and said a few words to Bud Peterson. Bud got into the back seat of the squad car with the cop and the car drove away. The sky was getting dark pretty fast and the crowd broke up.

One of Bud's sisters, Irma, the one who was twelve, had a dog, a brown and black mutt. I couldn't remember its name. Nobody had said anything about Irma's dog, if it got out alive or not. I used to see her walking that dog when I was coming home from baseball or football practice.

Bud Peterson went to live with a relative. Once in a while, in the first few weeks after the fire, I would see him back in the neighborhood, hanging out with the guys, then I didn't see him anymore. Somebody said he'd moved away from Chicago.

One morning, more than thirty years later, I was sitting at a bar in Paris drinking a coffee when, for no particular reason, I thought about standing in front of the Peterson house that afternoon and wondering: If it had been snowing hard enough the night before, could the snow have put out the fire? Then I remembered the name of Irma Peterson's dog.

Door to the River

Roy read in a science book about a parasite that lives in water and enters the skin of human beings, goes to the head and causes loss of sight. This condition, Roy learned, was sometimes called river blindness. Soon after he'd read this, Roy was taken on a Friday night by his cousin Ray to Rita's Can't Take It With You, a blues club on the West Side. Ray was twenty-two, six years older than Roy. Ray had recently enlisted in the Navy and wanted to celebrate before leaving for boot camp the following Monday. The cousins were accompanied to Rita's by Ray's friend Marvin Kitna, an accordionist in a polka band who had been to the club several times before.

"The Wolf's playing tonight," Kitna told Roy and Ray. "He's gettin' up there, but he's still the best."

Roy, Ray and Marvin Kitna were the only white patrons that night in Rita's Can't Take It With You. Kitna seemed to know almost everybody there, from the two bartenders, Earl and Lee, to many of the customers, as well as the two off-duty Chicago cops, Malcolm and Durrell, who were paid to provide security. Roy let his cousin and Kitna order beers and shots of Jim Beam for the three of them. The waitress, whom Marvin addressed as Dolangela, and who favored them with a dazzling dental display of gold and silver, did not ask any of them, even Roy, for verification of their ages.

Roy slowly sipped his beer and kept his mouth shut. He did not touch the shot of bourbon. The Wolf put on a great performance, crawling around on the stage, lying on his back while playing guitar and emitting his trademark howl. Ray and Marvin Kitna got up and danced a couple of times with girls Kitna knew. Roy was content to sit still and take in the show.

After the boys had been there for about an hour, a girl came over to their table, pulled up a chair and sat down between Roy and Ray.

"Hi," she said to Roy. "My name's Esmeraldina. What's yours?"

"Roy."

"You got beautiful hair, Roy. You mind do I touch it?"

"No."

Esmeraldina ran the fingers of her right hand through Roy's wavy black hair.

"You Eyetalian?" she asked him. "You an Eyetalian boy, huh?"

Roy shook his head. "I'm mostly Irish," he said.

"Pretty Eyetalian boy with turquoise eyes."

Esmeraldina draped her left arm around Roy's shoulders while she played with his hair.

"Just go along with her, Roy," said Marvin Kitna. "She won't bite."

"Oh yes, I do," Esmeraldina said. "I surely do can bite when a particular feelin' comin' on."

She poured Roy's shot of Beam into his glass of beer and picked up the glass.

"You mind do I take a taste?" she asked Roy.

Roy shook his head no and Esmeraldina drank half of the contents.

"What's that particular feelin' you're talkin' about, Esmeraldina?" asked Roy's cousin.

She grinned, revealing a perfect row of teeth unadorned by metal, and replied, "When a man get under my skin, crawl all up inside so's I can't itch it or see straight. Happens, I ain't responsible for myself, what I do until the feelin' wear off."

"How long's that take?" asked Marvin Kitna.

"Depends on the man," Esmeraldina said.

"Like river blindness," said Roy.

"What's that, honey?"

"A water bug swims in through a person's pores up to their head and makes them go blind."

Esmeraldina stared for a long moment into Roy's eyes, then she kissed him softly on the mouth.

"I bet you know all kinds of interestin' things, Roy," she said. "You want to dance with me?"

"Sure."

Esmeraldina picked up Roy's glass and finished off the shot and beer before they headed to the dance floor. Jimmie "Fast Fingers" Dawkins' "All for Business" was playing on the jukebox. She pressed her skinny body hard against Roy's and wrapped her arms around his back. Esmeraldina nudged him gently around in response to the slow blues. Roy guessed that Esmeraldina was in her early twenties but he didn't want to ask for fear she would in turn ask him how old he was and he did not want to have to lie.

"How old are you, Roy?"

"Old enough to be here," he said.

"You pretty sharp. Sharp and pretty."

"You're very pretty yourself, Esmeraldina."

After the record ended, Esmeraldina took Roy by the hand and led him out of the club. It was cold outside, too cold to be in the street without a coat. Roy had left his on the back of his chair at the table. Esmeraldina did not have one, either; she shivered in her short-sleeve blouse as she walked him to the right, around the corner onto Lake Street. A few yards ahead of them, two men, both wearing short-brimmed hats, were arguing with one another. One of them pulled a gun from a pocket and shot the other man in the forehead. The man who had been shot flew off his feet backwards as if he'd been caught off balance by Sugar Ray Robinson's quick left hook. The shooter ran and disappeared under the el tracks. Roy looked at the man on the ground: his eyes were open and his short-brim was still on his head.

"Bad timin'," Esmeraldina said. "We'd best go back indoors."

She and Roy hurried into Rita's Can't Take It With You, where Esmeraldina let go of him and lost herself in the crowd. Roy went over to the table where he'd been sitting with Ray and Marvin Kitna. They weren't there. Roy looked for them on the dance floor but he didn't see them. He took his jacket off the back of his chair and put it on. The music coming from the jukebox was very loud but Roy could hear a police siren. He saw Malcolm and Durrell, the security guards, go out the front door followed by Earl, one of the bartenders, and several customers. Roy ducked out, too, turned left and walked as fast as he could away from Lake

Street. He could still see the dead man with a nickel-sized hole above the bridge of his nose.

"How could his hat have stayed on?" Roy said.

Sailing in the Sea of Red He Sees a Black Ship on the Horizon

As a boy, Roy dreamed of going to sea, working as a deckhand on an oceangoing freighter, an ambition he was one day to realize. This vision took hold when he began reading the stories of Jack London and, later, those of Melville, Traven and Conrad. For awhile, he had a recurring dream in which he was a lookout positioned on the bow of a large boat at dawn. As the sun rose, the water turned red, and in the farthest distance Roy spotted an unmarked black cargo ship teetering on the lip of the horizon, as if it were precariously navigating a razor's edge of the planet. Roy felt that at any moment the mysterious freighter could tip over into the unseen and be lost forever.

When he was twelve years old, Roy's friend Elmo got his father to pay for him to take trumpet lessons. The old man operated a salvage business and didn't know much about music but he was proud of Elmo's desire to play the trumpet. The only tune Elmo ever learned to play all the way through, however, was "Twinkle, Twinkle, Little Star." Every so often, the old man would come home tired and dirty from the junkyard, plop down with a can of Falstaff in his favorite chair and ask Elmo to play something. Elmo would get his horn and stumble through "Twinkle, Twinkle, Little Star," which never failed to delight his father.

"How's the trumpet lessons goin', son?" the old man would ask him. "Makin' progress, Dad," Elmo would say. "Makin' progress."

When Elmo quit taking trumpet lessons, the old man was visibly disappointed. "Don't know why he stopped," he said, shaking his almost entirely bald head. "He was makin' progress."

Many years later, when Elmo's father learned that he was dying from stomach cancer, the old man refused to have chemotherapy. All he wanted was morphine, to dull the pain. The old man had been a Marine during World War II and had seen combat in the Pacific, where he'd contracted malaria, of which he still suffered occasional bouts. He told Elmo and Roy that war was stupid.

"War's a business, boys," said the old man, "big business, a way for the fat cats to make more coin when things ain't goin' so swift. This way they figure the ordinary citizen'll appreciate what they got and spend more after the shootin' stops. The fat cats live to make suckers out of us regular Joes."

Every day for the last six months of his life, the old man sat in a lawn chair in front of his garage and never complained, even when his burly body shrunk down to the size of a boy's. He was never mean; all the kids in the neighborhood liked him.

"I want to go out being who I am," he said, explaining why he refused to undergo chemotherapy.

After he passed away, Elmo called up Roy and said, "The old man died today. He's on that black ship you used to dream about."

"He was a great man," Roy told him.

"That's what I always thought," said Elmo.

ABOUT BARRY GIFFORD

Barry Gifford's novels have been translated into twenty-eight languages. His book *Night People* was awarded the Premio Brancati in Italy, and he has been the recipient of awards from PEN, the National Endowment for the Arts, the American Library Association, the Writers Guild of America, and the Christopher Isherwood Foundation. David Lynch's film *Wild at Heart*, which was based on Gifford's novel, won the Palme d'Or at the Cannes Film Festival in 1990, and his novel *Perdita Durango* was made into a feature film by Spanish director Alex de la Iglesia in 1997. Barry Gifford co-wrote with director David Lynch the film *Lost Highway* (1997); he also co-wrote with director Matt Dillon the film *City of Ghosts* (2003), as well as the libretto for Ichiro Nodaira's opera, *Madrugada* (2005). Mr. Gifford's most recent books include *The Phantom Father*, named a *New York Times* Notable Book of the Year; *Wyoming*, named a *Los Angeles Times* Novel of the Year, and which has been adapted for the stage and film; *The Sinaloa Story*; *The Rooster Trapped in the Reptile Room: A Barry Gifford Reader*; *Do the Blind Dream?*; and *The Stars Above Veracruz*. Mr. Gifford's writings have appeared in *Punch, Esquire, Rolling Stone, Sport*, the *New York Times, El Pais, El Universal, La Repubblica, Projections, La Nouvelle Revue Française* and many other publications. He lives in the San Francisco Bay Area. For more information please visit www.BarryGifford.com.